DATE DUE

Brett McCarthy: **Work in Progress**

Maria Padian

Alfred A. Knopf
New York

Visit us on the Web! www.randomhouse.com/teens

Educators and librarians, for a variety of teaching tools, visit us at www.randomhouse.com/teachers

The Library of Congress has cataloged the hardcover edition of this work as follows:
Padian, Maria.
Brett McCarthy : work in progress / Maria Padian.
        p. cm.
SUMMARY: Eighth-grader Brett McCarthy—once good student and best-friend-to-Diane, now suspended and friendless—faces school and family troubles as she grapples with her redefined life.
ISBN 978-0-375-84675-5 (trade) — ISBN 978-0-375-94675-2 (lib. bdg.) — ISBN 978-0-375-84940-4 (e-book)
[1. Grandmothers—Fiction. 2. Friendship—Fiction. 3. Interpersonal relations—Fiction. 4. Cancer—Fiction.
5. Junior high schools—Fiction. 6. Schools—Fiction. 7. Family life—Maine—Fiction.] I. Title.
PZ7.P1325Fo 2008
[Fic]—dc22
2007004415

ISBN 978-0-440-24055-6 (tr. pbk.)

Printed in the United States of America
October 2009
10 9 8 7 6 5 4 3 2 1

First Trade Paperback Edition

For **Madsy**

Acknowledgments

Writing has proved to be a far more solitary, challenging, and joyful process than I ever imagined. I would never have completed this book without the support and advice of so many, but especially:

My wise, enthusiastic agent, Edite Kroll, my fabulous editor, Nancy Hinkel, assistant editor Allison Wortche, and our wonderfully thorough copy editor, Renée Cafiero.

My intrepid readers, especially Charlotte Agell, Dan Elish, Elizabeth Owens, Christine Bolzan, and the Beacoms: Betsy, Kate, and Hannah.

My husband, Conrad Schneider, who always believes in me more than I believe in myself.

And above all, my daughter, Madeline, who was there every step of the way.

45 Definitions of Brett McCarthy

in·ter·lop·er

I've been obsessed lately with trying to pinpoint the exact moment when I got redefined.

That's one of my grandmother's favorite words. It basically means defined again. **Define** means *to make clear; mark the limits of; identify the essential qualities or meaning of.* Before my life changed from fairly decent to really bad, my self-definition was pretty straightforward.

Brett McCarthy: *Only Child; Only Granddaughter; Vocab Ace; Best Eighth-Grade Corner Kicker in Maine; Diane's Best Friend.*

Then came the redefinition.

Brett McCarthy: *Deadest Meat in Maine and Possibly the Planet; Practically Friendless; Violent; Suspended.*

Can you blame me for wanting to sort this out?

It all got started like any other day: at The Junior.

As in "Mescataqua Junior High School," the big green letters on the front brick wall. Kit was the one who noticed that every morning Diane stood directly under the word "Junior." Never under "Mescataqua," never under "School." But perfectly positioned between the "i" and "o" of "Junior," leaning against the wall, her backpack slung over one slender shoulder.

Diane insisted she wasn't doing it on purpose, but once Kit pointed it out, it got to be our thing. "See you at The Junior!" we'd say each afternoon, instead of "See you tomorrow!" Or "Meet me at The Junior!" if we planned to get together after school.

Diane, Kit, me, and (unfortunately) Jeanne Anne. Except for Jeanne Anne, the interloper, we'd known each other forever, from as far back as preschool. And even though we all had other friends outside the group, and sometimes got into really bad fights among ourselves, there was never any question about *us*. We were the first four chairs at the lunch table; the first four names on the Instant Messenger Buddy List; the first four numbers on speed dial.

Interloper: *intruder; interferer.* Someone who moves to Mescataqua in seventh grade and attaches herself to your BFF.

Within the group, Diane Pelletier was my first and best friend, even though she's nothing like me. For one thing, she's beautiful. She has licorice-shiny long black hair and lavender eyes. I have short frizzy hair that my mother describes as "strawberry blond." That's a nice term for "light brown with red highlights." Trust me, it's a noncolor.

Diane is really smart and really funny in a quiet way. I'm funny too, but in a loud, opinionated way. Diane can't catch or kick a ball without injuring herself. I'm totally into sports. Diane looks great in clothes, and people tend to copy what she wears. I'm a wrinkle magnet and break out in a stress rash when I enter a mall.

Despite all this she was my best. We slept over at each other's houses at least twice a month, talking all night. We agreed about most things. Except one. Diane was a little more tolerant and a lot more patient than I was when it came to jerks. Like Jeanne Anne.

For instance, on the morning of Monday, October 15th, she came rushing up to The Junior practically shaking with excitement. Kit was filling us in on what had happened during the previous night's episode of her favorite TV reality drama.

"You *guys*!" Jeanne Anne burst out, interrupting the story. "You are *not* going to believe this!"

"Good, then don't bother telling us," said Kit. She had just been describing the giant, maggot-like insects that members of Team A, on the verge of starvation in Fiji, were probably going to eat on the next episode. Kit tends to share my opinion of Jeanne Anne, and assumed that whatever she had to say was less interesting . . . and more annoying . . . than maggots.

"No, really," insisted Jeanne Anne. She faced Diane. "Diane, your telephone number is 555-1749, right?"

"Last time I checked." Diane smiled.

"Okay," Jeanne Anne said. She took one of her dramatic pauses. "Bob Levesque's number is 555-1748."

Blank stares. Silence. Finally broken by Kit.

"That's really fascinating, Jeanne Anne. Now back to the maggots . . ."

"Aah!" Jeanne Anne cried in exasperation. "Hello, people! Am I the only one who realizes what an amazing coincidence this is?"

"Yes, you are," replied Kit. The bell rang at this point, and we began moving toward the main entrance.

"Oh, c'mon!" Jeanne Anne pleaded. She was getting whiny now, and a little loud. People were turning to look at us. "Remember that thing you used to do with the phones? Don't pretend this isn't an awesome discovery!"

Even Diane realized it was time to shut her up. Broadcasting our old prank in the middle of the school lobby was not cool. Diane pulled Jeanne Anne close.

"Keep your voice down," she hissed. "We'll meet at study hall and talk about it."

Satisfied, Jeanne Anne smiled and headed off to her locker.

"Who told her about the Phone Thing?" I asked Diane as soon as Jeanne Anne was out of earshot. "And why is she looking up Bob Levesque's telephone number?"

"Oh . . . you know her!" Diane shrugged. "She's always crushin' on someone."

"She is a certifiable jerk. A complete idiot!" I sputtered.

I was upset. I get klutzy . . . and loud . . . when I'm upset.

So the "idiot" came out with a bit more volume than necessary, and at the same time I managed to smash my size-nine sneakers down on someone's toes.

"Ouch! Hey, watch it!"

The toes belonged to a pair of electric-blue eyes. The eyes went with some sun-bleached, tousled blond hair and perfect white teeth without a trace of orthodontia. In other words, I had just crushed the foot of none other than Bob Levesque, resident Greek God. And called him an idiot in the middle of a crowded hallway.

Bob looked at me and Diane, annoyed. Then, something . . . either my comically guilty expression or Diane's beautiful face . . . made him change his mind, because he grinned.

"An idiot! She called me an idiot! My heart is broken." Bob pressed his hands against his chest dramatically, closed his electric blues, and pretended to fall back in a theatrical faint. His ever-present posse of cool friends, who never seemed to miss one of his performances, laughed in appreciation. Before I could stammer out an "excuse me," Bob lurched out of view and disappeared in the sea of students.

Diane stared at me in shock.

"It's a sign," she whispered. "And you know, one digit off. That's almost too good to be true."

True, but as it turns out, not good.

ap·o·plec·tic

A little background is important at this point.

For starters, the Phone Thing was something the three of us had dreamed up years earlier. It was very elementary school, and we hadn't done it in ages. It meant calling people on the telephone and playing a joke on them. Not some dumb joke, but a truly creative prank that took more than just a little acting talent.

For example, a dumb joke would involve dialing a stranger and saying, "Hi, I'm from the power company. We're just calling to see if your refrigerator is running." Caught off guard, the stranger would reply, "Yes, it is." Then everyone would scream, "So run after it!"

That's a stupid joke, and we never lowered ourselves to such a level.

Our joke was slick, and our delivery perfect. So slick and so perfect, in fact, the person at the other end never even knew we'd fooled them. We could laugh ourselves sick at someone else's expense, but because they didn't know they'd been tricked, we never got caught . . . until Tuesday, October 16th.

A second bit of background: Bob Levesque. Bob is the son of a car dealership owner in our town. Levesque's Mescataqua Dodge. My dad says only in Maine, where the phone book is full of names like Ouellette and Thiboutot and the atlas is full of towns like Chesuncook and Norridgewock, can you get away with a mouthful like that. Dad's the sort of guy who notices those things: He's an English professor. Which may explain where I inherited my obsessive way with words.

Anyway, Bob's house sits atop a wide green lawn that slopes down to the ocean. His parents look ten years younger than everyone else's, and I once heard Diane's mother refer to them as "Ken and Barbie," even though their real names are Drew and Meredith.

If you had lined me and my friends up under The Junior and asked Bob Levesque who we were, I doubt he could have cared less. We did not exist on his planet or even circle in his orbit.

Until Tuesday, October 16th.

By study hall on Monday, Jeanne Anne was practically apoplectic.

Apoplectic: *highly excited.*

She couldn't make herself stop talking about Bob Levesque's phone number. Kit kept telling Jeanne Anne to lower her voice.

"You know, Jeanne Anne, we really don't do that anymore," Kit whispered, glancing over at study hall teacher at the front of the room. Students at other tables kept looking our way.

"*You* were in on the Phone Thing?" Jeanne Anne practically squealed. Study hall teacher's head shot up from the papers he was grading. "Why doesn't anyone ever tell me *anything?*"

"One guess," I muttered. Diane kicked me under the table.

"Ladies, do I need to separate you?" study hall teacher asked. Everyone opened books and pretended to read. After a few minutes of silence Diane quietly ripped a sheet from her binder, scribbled on it, and slid it into the middle of the table.

"Maybe once more . . . for old times' sake?" it read.

Jeanne Anne grabbed the pen from Diane's hand and scrawled "YES!" on top of the page. Kit rolled her eyes at me but added a "yes." Then she paused and wrote, "Foreign or domestic?" She handed the pen to me, and everyone waited. I was the final vote.

"Sworn to secrecy . . . *right?*" I wrote. Three heads nodded emphatically at me.

"We play Topsfield today. Levesque tomorrow?" I wrote. Three nods again.

"Foreign," I wrote.

"*Sí, señorita,*" Kit replied in a perfect Spanish accent. Study hall teacher's head jerked up and the bell rang at the same moment. We gathered our things, and as our crowd moved toward the door, I felt someone tap my shoulder. Michael.

"What was that all about?" he asked.

"Shut up." I smiled at him. "Aren't you supposed to be at your brainiac lessons?" I hung back so we could talk.

Michael is the school genius. He is definitely going to end up either as another Ken Jennings—that guy who won more than two million dollars on *Jeopardy!*—or as the next Steve Jobs, and invent something as cool as the iPod. He has a photographic memory, he speed-reads, and no math class can hold him. For a while they were shipping him out to the high school for math, but now someone from the college comes in and works with Michael.

I've known him since forever. Our dads were in grad school together, and both came to Mescataqua to teach at the college. When we were younger, our mothers started the joke about how we would probably end up married to each other, but I told them that would be incest.

Sometimes I get the creepy feeling that Michael would be okay with the idea, but since he hasn't tried anything stupid, like holding my hand or something, things are cool.

"So, your grandmother and I have big plans for tomorrow afternoon," Michael said.

"Let me guess," I said. "You're going to put a parachute on an old bicycle and ride it off the roof?"

"Guess again."

"You're going to construct a nuclear reactor out of the broken vacuum cleaner she picked up last week?"

"Close."

I sighed. Usually I didn't mind playing this game with Michael, but at that moment I had other things on my mind.

"I give up. Just tell me," I said.

"Nope," he replied. "You've got to come by and see for yourself." He took a sharp right down the corridor and ducked into his last-period class. I didn't have a chance to tell him that I had other plans for that afternoon.

As it turns out, reassembling old vacuum cleaner parts with my grandmother and the captain of the school math team would have been a much better choice.

glow•er

Monday, October 15th, my soccer team played Topsfield, our archrivals. Most of the time our games are attended by a handful of parents and a few students, but Topsfield games are different. Gazillions of fans turn out, for both sides.

For one thing, Topsfield is right next door, so it's a short drive either way. For another thing, Mescataqua and Topsfield are soccer-crazed towns, each with rival private soccer clubs and state-championship high school teams. When the Topsfield Buccaneers take on the Mescataqua Maineiacs, expect blood. Hysterical parents screaming from the sidelines. Coaches bellowing. Refs handing out yellow cards. Players hitting the dirt. Hard.

For me, Topsfield meant one thing: Big Joan. Big Joan Biff, to be exact. A five-foot-nine, 155-pound eighth grader who could run the length of the field with the speed . . . and impact . . . of a linebacker. Joan had the build, single-mindedness, and intellect of a Mack truck, and those who

11

valued their skeletal systems stepped aside when Joan drove the ball. She'd never gotten a red card, but she averaged one yellow per game. Of course, everyone knew she'd gladly take a red card if it meant clocking Brett McCarthy.

Basically, she hated me. At the season's opener in September I had humiliated Big Joan before throngs of her adoring fans. No match for her power, I could, however, out-finesse and out-think her from my position at midfield. So six times, as she barreled toward our goal, snorting and steaming, I had stripped the ball from her and sent it sailing ahead to Kit, our center striker. Kit went on to score five out of those six times (we won, 5–3), and before it was over, people from the Mescataqua side of the field were cheering for "Brett the Biffolator." It was sweet. Until we had to line up and do the "good game" handshakes.

Big Joan was waiting. She stood at the end of the Bucs' line, glowering, and if I'd seen her murderous expression, I'd have been better prepared for what was coming.

Glower: *to stare or look at someone with anger.*

When I reached Joan, I stuck my hand out, palm open, prepared to gently slap hers in return.

"Good game, good ga—YOUCH!" I screamed as Joan wound up and torpedoed her fist into the bones of my hand. Pain exploded from my fingertips clear to my elbow.

Kit, behind me in line, was the first to react. As Joan lumbered away with the rest of the Bucs, Kit whirled on her, outraged.

"What was that for? Hey, come back here, you big ape!" With a flying leap Kit sprang on her. It looked like a Chihuahua attacking a St. Bernard, which is saying something, because Kit's no shrimp. In a nanosecond other girls took up the cry, and before you knew it, half the Mescataqua Maineiacs and the Topsfield Buccaneers were in the dirt, while I was doubled over holding my hand. When it was over, four players, two from each team, ended up with suspensions. Ironically, Joan and Kit were not among them.

Monday, October 15th, was the first time our two teams had met since The Brawl, as it came to be known. Fans turned out in big numbers. As I stood at my position at midfield, waiting for the ref to blow the starting whistle, I looked around. The sidelines were packed three deep. At one end a group of Mescataqua students had painted signs in green that read BIFF HER, BRETT! and were chanting accordingly. My nerves felt like tightly stretched piano wire. I turned to the center of the field and saw her.

Big Joan was scraping the turf with her cleats, like a bull. Topsfield had won the toss, and she stood in center kickoff position. Her eyes were locked on the Biffolator, and when our gazes finally met, she stopped her pawing, raised one arm, and pointed, wordlessly, at me.

I'm going to die, I thought as the whistle blew.

Joan touched the top of the ball with her foot and sprinted directly toward me. The girl to her left picked up the ball while the Topsfield front line took off. It was the standard

Topsfield opening play: They'd pass to their wing, center to Joan, who'd drive uncontested for a goal. Topsfield won most of their games by doing this over and over. The key was stopping the wing, because once Joan got the ball, the play was pretty much complete. Unless, of course, I stole it from her.

As I backpedaled, Kit struggled to strip the ball from the Topsfield girl, both of them leaning hard into each other. Kit managed to tap it away, spin off the girl, and take up the dribble toward their goal. Yes! I thought. Things were already looking better.

That's what I was thinking when my legs went out from under me and I was airborne. Joan! I thought, the second before I hit the ground. I'd never seen her coming. Neither had the ref, although plenty of fans had seen her stick her leg out and trip me. But there was so much screaming going on, the refs didn't hear the shrieks for a card. I rolled over, winded but otherwise unhurt, and looked straight up into Big Joan's jowly face.

"I think you've just been Biffed," she sneered before she ran off.

Here's the thing about playing against Mescataqua Junior High School: Don't get Brett McCarthy motivated. I don't know, maybe I've got an adrenaline disorder or something. But when I'm fired up, I enter this zone and get beyond aggressive. It's like I'm bionic or a predator, the ball is dinner, and I haven't eaten in three days. Watch out.

I leaped up and tore after her. Kit and the other members of our front line were passing the ball back and forth, trying to maneuver into scoring position. The Topsfield defense was playing pretty far up, an attempt to draw them offsides. Big Joan had stopped just beyond the midfield line, waiting for a pass. She had her back to me, and despite my bionic focus I could hear the crowds roar as I drew close.

"Pass back!" I screamed as I whipped past Joan and hurtled toward the goal. A Mescataqua player tapped the ball back to me. There were no defenders in sight as I wound up and booted it high, a giant arc over our front line, the Topsfield fullbacks, and the goalie, who leaped into the air waving her hands. That beautiful black-and-white-spotted ball floated inches below the top metal bar of the goal and swished into the net. One to nothing.

As people screamed wildly along the sidelines and my teammates rushed up to high-five me, I looked for Big Joan. She was trudging slowly across the grass, back to starting position. When she was about ten paces away, I cleared my throat loudly, and she looked up.

I raised my arm, pointed at her, and held it there for five full seconds. Noise erupted on the sidelines.

The final score on Monday, October 15th, when the Mescataqua Maineiacs played the Topsfield Buccaneers, was 4–1. Kit headed two goals in off my corner kicks. I scored once more, a kind of ball-hoggy move when I should have passed off but decided to drive hard to the goal and laser it inches away from the goalie's hands. Big Joan racked up one goal on the standard Topsfield play. Boring.

When the final whistle blew, my teammates did something they'd never done before. They grabbed me and Kit and hoisted us to their shoulders. Fans streamed onto the field, and as Kit and I grabbed hands, laughing hysterically at the crazy scene, our teammates chanted, "Biffolators! Biffolators! Biff Biff Biffolators!"

My eyes scanned the throng. Mom was in the stands, and she blew kisses at me. Diane was there, jumping up and down like an excited electron, waving at us. "You rock, girl!" I heard her yell. I saw Jeanne Anne standing a little off to one side. She was talking to a couple of girls I didn't know, and unlike the rest of the universe, she wasn't shouting and jumping. When I happened to catch her looking my way, her expression surprised me.

I'd call it . . . annoyed. No, more than that. Pissed off. It seemed so out of place, because everyone else was really pumped. Then I realized I'd seen that face before. On Big Joan Biff, back in September.

The glower.

met·a·phor

Tuesday, October 16th. Coach gave us a day off practice, a gift for the big Topsfield win. So when the final bell rang, we met at The Junior, then headed to Diane's, which is only a short walk from school.

The Pelletiers' house is huge. An immense maze of perfectly decorated rooms connected by long hallways and short flights of stairs, it's a work in progress. Mr. Pelletier is a builder and Mrs. Pelletier an interior decorator, and over the years their house has become an experiment of sorts as they keep adding rooms or tearing out features they don't like anymore.

Mrs. Pelletier is big into color. Once, Diane had come home from school to find her bedroom emptied and a work crew painting her walls "eggplant" (basically purple) with "lime" (a.k.a. green) trim. I remember being astonished at how calm she was.

"Didn't you get even a *little* annoyed?" I asked when she

told me about the eggplant. "I mean, shouldn't you have some say about the color of your own room?"

Diane had shrugged. "I guess I don't care about that sort of stuff like you do," she said. "I mean, it's just paint, and Mom repaints rooms once a month. Besides"—she smiled slyly—"I got to sleep in the den while it dried. I watched cable until two."

When we arrived at the Pelletiers', Diane's mother greeted us at the door. A suspiciously large smile stretched across her face, which worried me. No mother, unless she has something up her sleeve, looks that happy when she discovers four eighth graders on her doorstep.

"Perfect timing, girls!" she exclaimed. "I was just ducking out to the store with Merrill. But now I have *four* babysitters to keep an eye on him!"

Merrill, the Nine-Year-Old Menace of Mescataqua, rarely had babysitters. The Pelletiers had run out of teenagers willing to put up with him. They'd managed to snag Jeanne Anne for one night, back when she first moved in last year and didn't know his rep. But now, despite her constant sucking up to Diane, even she refused to babysit Merrill.

"Oh, Mom, no, please," Diane began pleading. "We were going to study. We have a *big* test tomorrow. We won't get anything done with Merrill bugging us!"

Of course, Mrs. Pelletier wasn't fooled. She made a beeline for her car, never breaking stride and waving to us over her head as she hurried out.

"He's watching TV," she called over her shoulder. "Help

yourselves to snacks. And study hard, girls!" She waved, then honked as she pulled away.

"C'mon," Diane sighed. "Let's see where he is."

We found Merrill seated on the floor in the den, a few feet from the flat-screen television, hypnotically shoveling fistfuls of orange goldfish-shaped crackers into his mouth from an enormous bowl in his lap. He was watching a video, and the four of us stared uneasily at the unusual phenomenon of Merrill Sitting Still.

"Shh," whispered Diane, ushering us away from the den and toward the kitchen. "He's good like that for thirty minutes. We'll use the phone in the guest bedroom, and he won't even notice us."

Diane loaded us up with Sprite and Oreos, which we carried to a blue ("sea glass") bedroom at the other end of the house. I seated myself at the head of the bed, near the phone.

"You know, I've been thinking," said Kit. "I'll bet the Levesques have caller ID."

Everyone was silent. In the early days of the Phone Thing, caller ID was rare. These days it was more prevalent, and the Levesques were pretty likely to have whatever was prevalent. This was a problem. If someone could see where the call originated, the prank wouldn't work.

Diane snapped her fingers.

"Cell phone," she said, and dashed out of the room. She returned a minute later with a small, electric-blue phone, which fit neatly into the palm of her hand.

"Oh, you are *so* lucky!" Jeanne Anne exclaimed. "That's a Nouveau 3300! I have been *begging* for one of those!"

"That's *yours?*" I asked, stunned. Since when does your BFF get a cell phone and you don't know? Diane didn't meet my eyes.

"Early birthday present." She shrugged. She plopped beside me on the bed, held the tiny receiver button-side up, and expertly depressed the on button. The phone lit with a green glow when it located a signal. "Just dial," she said, handing it to me.

"Okay," I sighed. "Quiet on the set."

"What if Bob answers?!?" Jeanne Anne suddenly squealed, hurling herself backward on the bed in excitement and practically bouncing me onto the floor.

I calmly hit the end button. I turned to Diane, who recognized the warning signs on my face.

"People who can't control themselves have to leave," I said.

"Okay, okay!" Jeanne Anne huffed, popping back up. "Lighten up, Brett."

Diane's pleading eyes, begging me to *not* lose it with Jeanne Anne, kept me under control. Only Diane knew how close I had been in recent months to telling Jeanne Anne off. Frankly, I just didn't get it. Back when she arrived in Mescataqua last year, she'd attached herself to us like a barnacle to a boat's bottom. Kit and I didn't want to be mean, but we were like, Huh? We couldn't figure out why someone who pasted pictures of Brad Pitt in her locker and went for monthly pedicures at Nail World wanted to hang with us. I mean, I love Brad as much as the next girl, but *locker pinups*?

I'd tried to explain all this to Diane, but she didn't want to hear it. Sometimes I suspected Diane even liked her.

I took a deep breath and picked up the phone again.

"Shoot," I said.

"555-1748," Diane prompted. I punched the numbers into the keypad, hit send, and waited.

"It's ringing," I said quietly.

"Hello?" A woman's voice. Mrs. Levesque.

"Hey, Mom," I said cheerfully. "I'm ready to be picked up."

"Oh." There was a hesitant pause at the other end. "I'm sorry. I think you have the wrong number."

"Isn't this 555-1749?" I replied quickly, giving her the Pelletiers' number.

"No, but you're close," she laughed. "This is 1748. Sorry."

"Oh, no. Wait. Wait, please don't hang up!" I exclaimed in a panicky voice.

"Yes?" the woman replied.

"Um, ma'am? I was supposed to call my mom when it was time to come get me." A pause.

"Come get you where, dear?" asked Mrs. Levesque.

"I'm at the movie theater and . . . hello? Are you still there?" I shouted into the phone.

"Yes, I'm here! What is it?" replied Mrs. Levesque.

"Oh, great! Listen . . . I think my cell phone is running out of juice. Would you call my mom for me and tell her I'm ready to get picked up? Tell her I'll wait for her out front?"

"Oh gosh, honey, sure!" said Mrs. Levesque. "That's no problem."

She was really nice. Super nice. From somewhere deep in the dark recesses of my conscience I could feel a slight prickle of guilt. Unfortunately, I pushed the prickle aside.

"Now, which theater are you at, and what's your name?" she said. She was all mom: taking charge, making it right.

"Hello!" I shouted again. "I'm losing the signal . . . are you still there?"

"Yes, dear," Mrs. Levesque shouted back. "Quick, what's your number?"

"555-1748," I said. "I'm Josephine. I'm at Hoyt's . . ." Mid-sentence I cut the phone off. No more juice. I turned to Kit.

"You're on," I grinned.

There was no containing the whoops. Who was it? Who answered? What did they say? Everyone seemed to be asking at once. We almost didn't hear the phone ring.

"Shh! Shh! Everyone, quiet!" Diane demanded. Kit slid into my spot. She wiggled her shoulders and shook out her hair. It reminded me of the way divers loosen up before plunging into the pool, or the way an actor warms up before a performance.

Kit picked up on the third ring.

"'Ello?" she said tentatively into the receiver. She paused as Mrs. Levesque spoke.

"*Sí, sí*, Josephine," Kit replied, nodding her head, as if she were engaged in a real conversation. Totally in character. After a few seconds, Kit interrupted.

"*Pero, señora*," Kit said. "No English. *Hablo español*." Kit paused, listening. If Mrs. Levesque answered in Spanish, Kit might have to bail. I knew she could imitate a Spanish accent and manage a few words, but to actually conduct a conversation in Spanish would be way out of her league. We all held our breaths.

Kit smiled and flashed us a thumbs-up. Mrs. Levesque was sticking to English. We were still on.

"*No comprendo*," Kit said. "*No hablo inglés, señora*. I. Clean. House." Kit spoke these last three words with the slow emphasis of a well-practiced, unfamiliar phrase. Kind of the way we memorized dialogues for Spanish classes, only half understanding what we said.

At this point, having played her role of the non-English-speaking cleaning lady, Kit was supposed to hang up. That's how the Phone Thing worked. You involved the person in a made-up mini-crisis—Josephine waiting for a ride home, Josephine forgetting her cleats before the big soccer game, something like that—and convinced the person to call "home" for Josephine, where the non-English-speaking maid was the only adult available.

We never knew what happened after the call ended.

We didn't care; it was immensely funny to us that they even bought it in the first place and bothered to call back. Once Kit did her maid thing and hung up, the prank was over.

But this time Kit didn't hang up. She listened. For too long. Diane began making a chopping motion with her hand, signaling Kit to cut it off. Meanwhile, the expression on Kit's face began to change. Her eyes got big. Panicky. Uh-oh, I thought. Barbie just threw her a curve. The prickle in my stomach became a burn.

"No!" Kit suddenly burst out, sounding very much like her old American self. Something had gone wrong.

"No English, *señora*," Kit quickly countered. "I clean house. *Adíos*." She slammed the phone onto its cradle as if the receiver were red-hot.

"What just happened?" Jeanne Anne demanded. "What's going on?"

"She's driving to Hoyt's to get Josephine," Kit said weakly. "She's concerned."

"Oh, no!" groaned Diane. "That's not supposed to happen." We looked at each other silently, stupidly. Then we totally broke up. Diane laughed so hard she began to gasp; Kit shrieked that she was going to pee in her pants and ran for the bathroom. I pictured Mrs. Levesque cruising the parking lot of Hoyt's Cineplex in her Lexus SUV, gazing worriedly out the window, and lost it to a fit of giggles.

Naturally, Jeanne Anne threw cold water on the whole thing.

"You know, you guys? *Guys!*" she said loudly. Diane was wiping her eyes. I was lying on the floor. Kit had emerged from the bathroom with a not-happy look on her face and was trying to say something, but Jeanne Anne had our attention.

"You know, that is *really* sweet of her," Jeanne Anne said.

"No, it's really *stupid* of her!" I countered loudly, and Diane and I burst out laughing again.

"Hey, everybody, shut up a minute . . . ," Kit began, but Jeanne Anne cut her off.

"No, it's really, really sweet," she persisted. "It's really nice that she'd go out of her way to help some kid she doesn't even know."

"Oh, brother," I muttered. Jeanne Anne turned and spoke directly to me.

"Maybe that's just something you wouldn't understand, Brett. You know? People being nice?"

"Okay, Jeanne Anne, what's your point?" Diane said. She could tell that once again Jeanne Anne and I were headed toward dangerous ground.

Jeanne Anne took a deep breath.

"I think we should call her back. Tell her the whole thing was a joke so she doesn't waste her time driving to Hoyt's."

Cries of no-way-are-you-out-of-your-mind? filled the sea-glass bedroom. Every one of us had at least a dozen good reasons why we shouldn't call the Levesques again, but Jeanne Anne would hear none of it. Before we could stop her, she'd picked up Diane's phone and dialed. Next thing we knew, she was speaking into the receiver.

"Uh, hi. Hi. Is this the Levesque residence?" A pause.

"Um . . . is your mother at home? May I speak to her?" Another pause. Kit, Diane, and I watched in horrified silence. I remember thinking, This is what it's like to watch a train wreck, or an accident on the highway. It's unreal, awful, and fascinating all at once.

"Oh. Do you know where she went?" Jeanne Anne continued. "Right. Okay. Listen, I know this is going to sound weird, but do you have any way to reach her? I mean, does she have a cell phone? Good. Well, I need you to call her and tell her there is no Josephine. Tell her I'm really, really sorry, but it was just a joke, and there is no Josephine at the movie theater." Jeanne Anne paused, listening. Then her face got all funny, with the nose all wrinkly. At first I thought she smelled something bad, but then I could see—she was smiling.

"No, I . . . I can't say who's calling. Is this Bob?" she said.

"Are you *nuts*!?" burst from my mouth. Certifiable jerk. Idiot. Boy-crazy idiot who didn't realize what sort of trouble we could get into if she opened her big mouth. Time to cut this off, I thought. So I made a Spider-Man-like leap at Jeanne Anne, hoping to yank the glowing blue phone from her hand.

Unfortunately, I'm no Spider-Man. Midleap I tripped on the bedspread and landed on the night table. A tan pottery lamp crashed to the floor. Diane exclaimed, "Oh, no!" and from the blue phone, which Jeanne Anne held away from her ear, we could hear a boy's voice loudly demanding, "What was that?"

I swung around and faced Jeanne Anne.

"Hang up. *Now*," I whispered in my most threatening way.

Then Jeanne Anne did two things that really surprised me. First, she stared me down. She looked me right in the eye with a glower that said in no uncertain terms, "Drop dead." I don't know why I had never seen it before, but Jeanne Anne had about as much use for me as I had for her.

Then she did the second thing. Returning the phone to her ear, her eyes locked on mine, Jeanne Anne spoke carefully into the receiver.

"Hello, Bob? Tell your mom it was Brett McCarthy who called. Tell her McCarthy thinks she's really funny." Jeanne Anne hit end.

That's when I heard it: a toilet flushing. Like marionette puppets suspended from a single string, we all turned our heads toward the sound. Which would turn out to be a metaphor for my soon-to-be-redefined life.

Metaphor: *an object or thing used in place of another to suggest a likeness between them.*

Merrill stood in the doorway of the sea-glass guest bathroom, orange powdered cheese ringing his mouth. Kit stood alongside him, shaking her head.

"I tried to warn you," she said. "He's been in the bathroom

most of the time. He snuck in." Merrill, quiet for once in his life. Sensing, with his sixth sense for trouble, that we were up to no good. Now he stood there, eyes wide, gazing from the broken lamp to our guilty faces. He grinned.

"I'm telling," Merrill said.

de·ba·cle

The scene at the Pelletiers' ended badly.

"Merrill!" Diane yelled. He bolted from the room, Diane in pursuit. "If you say one word to Mommy, I will make you *so* sorry!"

Jeanne Anne, meanwhile, hadn't moved from the bed. She'd carefully placed the cell phone on the night table, and now she bent over to retrieve a shard of pottery lamp from the floor. She seemed remarkably calm for a person left alone with two angry Biffolators.

"You jerk," I breathed, taking a step toward her. Kit moved between us.

"Give it a rest, Brett," Jeanne Anne snapped. "You don't scare me."

"That's because you're stupid!" I shouted. "If you had half the sense of a prune pit, you'd be pretty scared right now!" Kit put one hand on my shoulder and squeezed.

"Chill," she muttered in my ear. Jeanne Anne laughed.

"Ooh! Ouch! That hurts . . . a prune pit! Now I'm *really* gonna cry." She stood up, tossed the pottery shard on the bed, and glared at us. "For someone who's supposed to be good with words, that's pretty weak, McCarthy."

"Yeah? Well, I've got some more for you," I began. Kit put her hands up.

"Chill! Both of you!" she yelled.

"Why is she even here?" I demanded, looking at Kit. "Why is this . . . person . . . breathing in the same room as us?"

"Hello? Why the hell are *you* here?" Jeanne Anne retorted. "I'll tell you why. It's because *you're* too stupid to realize you aren't wanted anymore. I was invited; you refuse to leave."

This caught me up short. Who didn't want me anymore? Was she talking about Diane?

"Invited?" I exclaimed. "I'd just as soon invite a zit. Come to think of it, that's what you are. A zit. Unwanted, ugly, and hard to get rid of."

That got her. Jeanne Anne took a step toward me.

"Okay, enough. Enough!" Kit shouted. "Prune pit . . . zit . . . whatever . . . you need to leave. Now." She stared pointedly at Jeanne Anne, who, showing some sense for once in her life, quickly left the house. But not before shrieking that Kit and I were both losers.

It was a debacle.

Debacle: *a violent disruption; a complete failure; a great disaster.*

Following disasters I usually retreat to the same place: Nonna's house.

My maverick, almost-live-in Nonna is my dad's mom. My grandfather died when dad was little. Nonna never remarried, although she does have a "special friend," Mr. Beady, the most annoying old man on the planet.

"Maverick" is Nonna's word. When I was little, I imagined it meant she was a professional recycler. That's because Nonna collects used junk, cleans it up, fixes what's broken, and sells it all at her annual Super-Sized Garage Sale. Only recently did "maverick" appear on one of my vocabulary lists.

Maverick: *an unbranded range animal; esp. a motherless calf.*

Luckily, there was a second definition.

Maverick: *an independent individual who refuses to conform with his group.*

I like that, actually. I like to think of my Nonna as a rebel, especially since we McCarthys are pretty ordinary: a mom who quilts (a.k.a. a "fiber artist"), a college-professor dad, and a word-obsessed jock living in a midcoast Maine town. Nonna keeps us from being too boring.

From Halloween to Memorial Day she lives in a little rented house on the lot behind ours. Actually, it's minuscule. It looks like a playhouse, with small shutters and doors, and its roof slopes into funny angles, which is why we call it the Gnome Home. But it's perfect for Nonna, especially because it includes a detached two-car garage that she uses as a workshop and storage area for her yard sale.

The other five months, a.k.a. from the beginning of Black Fly Season to the end of the Tourist Season, Nonna spends at her ten-acre personal paradise, Spruce Island.

For non-Mainers the idea of a personal island probably seems outrageous, unless you're Bill Gates or something. And "paradise" is a relative term. One man's bliss is another man's Alcatraz. That's what Nonna says, usually after escorting un-appreciative visitors from the island. One rainy weekend, as old friends from Boston were unloading their wheeled suit-cases and paper shopping bags onto the dock, one commented that he felt like he'd just made it through an episode of *Survivor*.

For us McCarthys, on the other hand, a Spruce Island weekend hauling water cranked from a hand pump, sleeping on bunks in rough wooden cabins, and peeing in an outhouse, is the very definition of paradise.

October 16th usually found the Gnome Home vacant, its windows with their curtains drawn, like sleeping eyes. Nonna would have been on the island wrapping things up for the sea-son. Harvesting the last vegetables from her garden. Picking buckets of rose hips and boiling them into jam. Shuttering the cottages and wedging steel wool under the doors to discourage . . . although she could never completely prevent . . . mice. Once she'd packed up tight for the winter, Dad and I and (unfortunately) Mr. Beady, who has a pickup truck, would ferry her back to the mainland and Mescataqua.

But this year she'd returned early. She said she was tired and had an itchy brown-tail moth rash. As I walked from Diane's house the afternoon of October 16th, I was more than a little glad to know she had returned to the Gnome Home.

Because in the world of Brett McCarthy Screwups, this was big. It was worse than chewing gum in study hall, or a bad grade, or a trip to the principal's office.

It was death. Social death. From the lunchroom to the hallways to the playing fields of Mescataqua Junior High School—anywhere that Bob Levesque and his legion of cool friends existed—I was dead meat.

I would have to break the news to my parents that we had to move, or I had to transfer to private school.

As I approached the edge of the woods near Nonna's yard, I could hear little kids' voices and clapping, as if a birthday party were in full swing. I heard Nonna's voice above the others: "Okay, everyone, here it goes!"

There was a soft, percussive sound, a pop like old-fashioned musket fire. Then something moved in the trees above my head, whipping through the leaves. I heard it hit, splat, then rain down in bits. Gray, mushy, bad-smelling bits that landed around and on me. Perfect.

As I stepped out of the woods, I heard cheers. Across the clearing, in Nonna's backyard, a group of kids were arranged in chairs, like a viewing audience. Nonna was standing about twenty paces away from them, and with her, unmistakably, was Michael. They were holding a long white tube . . . PVC pipe . . . in a green plastic garbage can. They saw me step out of the woods.

"Brett!" Nonna called excitedly. "Come see our Potato Bazooka!"

ba·zoo·ka

Although one can find Potato Bazookas, also known as Hair Spray Spud Guns, on the Internet, complete with directions on how to build and operate them, bazookas are particularly prevalent in The County, a.k.a. Aroostook County, in northern Maine, where the world's best potatoes grow. Some might argue that Idaho potatoes are superior, but Mainers understand that no self-respecting potato would ever come from an "I" state.

Bazooka: *a light, portable weapon consisting of a smoothbore firing tube that launches armor-piercing rockets.* And potatoes. And just about anything else that fits.

Not only does The County produce awesome potatoes, it produces them in quantity. Tons. In such great numbers that people can't eat them . . . or sell them . . . fast enough. So for fun they make bazookas and blast them.

Nonna first learned of this from a County friend who would entertain her with stories of family potato-blasting

35

contests. One especially memorable competition began after dinner on Christmas Day and ended only after some enterprising and not-very-sentimental brothers had filled a bazooka with every ornament from the tree and shot them in a tinselly barrage across the snow-covered front yard.

People from The County, Nonna was convinced, knew how to have some big fun.

So Nonna had long yearned to build a bazooka of her own. Now, seeing Michael with her in the yard, it all made sense. This was what he had been talking about after study hall.

As I drew closer, I recognized the assembled group. A few hundred yards down the road a woman named Kathy Livingston ran a home day care . . . Miss Kathy's . . . for preschool-aged children. Visits to "see Mrs. McCarthy" were a regular part of the "curriculum." Basically, Kathy Livingston hired young women (Dad called them all the Kathies) to watch other people's kids, and when they got sick of TV, they brought the whole crew over to Nonna's, where there was always something interesting going on.

As I crossed the lawn, I saw about half a dozen little kids sitting in plastic molded chairs. Each held a potato.

"Who wants to show Brett how we make potatoes fly?" Nonna asked them. Little hands shot up excitedly. Nonna pointed to a tiny blond girl. She jumped off her chair and skipped confidently to the bazooka.

"Now," the girl said, as if I were the student and she were

the teacher, "first you drop in the potato." She reached up on tiptoe and deposited her potato in the pipe.

"Then you unscrew the bottom." Michael stepped forward and removed a cap from the bottom of the PVC pipe.

"Then you spray the hair spray into the bottom while you count to four," she continued, looking at Michael expectantly. He grabbed a can and began spraying. "One! Two! Three! Four!" Miss Kathy's kids all shouted. Michael quickly re-screwed the base cap.

"Fire!" the little girl squealed in delight.

Michael pressed a small ignition key, creating, I guessed, a tiny spark inside the pipe, which ignited the hair spray. There was a pop, and we all watched the potato shoot from the pipe and make a graceful arc overhead, landing in a dramatic ex-plosion of brown and white. Baked, I thought. Of course, it was just my luck to have gotten sprayed with a rotten one.

The kids and the Kathies cheered. I managed a half-hearted clap. On any other day this would have been totally awesome, but I was still recovering from the debacle at Diane's.

Just then a horn sounded from the driveway.

"Okay, everybody, time to go!" Nonna announced, waving her arms in a flocking motion, as if the children were geese. After whines for please-just-one-more, and repeated, enthusi-astic thank-yous from the Kathies, the group headed toward the driveway and the waiting van. Only Michael and I re-mained, the bazooka between us.

"You know," he said thoughtfully, "I don't get the impression that you fully appreciate the power and potential of the Potato Bazooka."

I sighed and flopped into one of the empty chairs.

"No, I do. Really, it's cool. I'm just a little distracted is all."

Michael gave me one of his "Yeah, right" looks before turning away and rummaging through a large cardboard box under the picnic table.

"I know just the thing to convince you," he said. Reaching deep into the box, he pulled something out.

"Ladies and gentlemen," he said, circus-ringmaster-style, "for your entertainment this afternoon we are thrilled to present the one, the only . . ." Michael spun around and with a flourish held up a plastic doll about a foot high, wearing a colorful outfit.

"Bazooka Barbie!" Michael cried.

"Oh my god," I said. "You're so weird." Doing voice imitations, especially from movies, is one of Michael's many Gifted and Talented tricks. He practically memorizes films and can quote whole scenes.

"We've seen her shop 'til she drops! Drive outrageous plastic sports cars! And wear more pink sequins than the surgeon general generally recommends for her continued health and safety! But today, ladies and gentlemen, Barbie will reach . . . literally . . . new heights of daring and fame as she explodes from this bazooka and flies out of sight! Madam!"

Michael held the doll out to me. A tousled wreck of

bleachy blond hair framed her head like a halo. She wore little pink-and-orange shorts, gray with dirt, and a matching T-shirt.

"Madam," Michael continued dramatically, "would you do the honors?"

Oh, whatever, I thought. Despite the day's debacle I was still mildly curious to see a Barbie burst over the backyard. I took her from Michael and positioned her arms up and over her head so that she would soar, Superman-style, into the trees.

Michael stood on one side of the bazooka; I stood on the other. He pulled the PVC pipe from the garbage can and unscrewed the base.

"You may load the Barbie as I inject the fuel," he said, holding the pipe level with the ground. I slid Barbie down the front end. Her smiling face and outstretched arms disappeared. Michael grabbed a can of Aqua Net off the picnic table and began spraying into the base, counting to himself, "One one-thousand, two one-thousand." At four he rescrewed the base cap and pointed the pipe skyward.

"To infinity, and beyond!" Michael shouted, Buzz Lightyear–style, and depressed the ignition button.

Barbie blasted from the bazooka in a flash of pink and orange. Her trajectory was high but short. She landed on the lawn with a bounce, somersaulting twice before coming to a stop a few feet from the woods' edge.

"Hmmm," Michael said, thoughtfully. "I wonder why the

potatoes went so much farther than the Barbie?" Even fooling around, Michael thinks and asks questions like a scientist.

We ran over to inspect her. Barbie had bent in the middle to form a perfect L. Her arms still extended over her head, but she had landed with her face planted in the grass. Her minuscule little butt, wrapped in its hot-pink, slightly singed shorts, pointed skyward.

"Barbie, that's not very ladylike," said Michael.

I couldn't help it—I howled. It felt good to laugh, even at poor Barbie's expense.

"I see now that you do not underestimate the power of the Potato Bazooka," Michael said in his Darth Vader voice.

"Let's do it again," I suggested, "this time *riding* a potato." We rescued Barbie from her undignified position and turned back to the house. Standing next to the bazooka, arms folded across her chest, stood my mother.

"Brett," she called across the lawn, "you need to come home. Now." Michael gave me a puzzled look.

"That doesn't sound too good," he said. I handed him Bazooka Barbie. She had green grass stains on her forehead.

"It's not," I said.

fore·bod·ing

Mom goose-stepped across the lawn and straight into the kitchen. I had just seen a movie in social studies about the rise to power of Adolf Hitler, and it included footage of goose-stepping soldiers saluting the Nazi flag, so I knew the march. If that wasn't foreboding enough, she didn't offer me a snack or ask her usual cheery how-was-school-today questions.

Foreboding: *predicting a coming ill or misfortune.* In other words, the future doesn't look bright.

"So," she began. "I just got a call from Marie Pelletier."

Merrill! I thought. That little brat.

"What do you think she told me, Brett?"

Mom had decided to dispense with the SS treatment and do her Spanish Inquisition thing. Instead of just blasting me with what-were-you-thinking-of's, she would pull it out of me with tortuous questions. I decided to just get it over with.

"Mom, it was an accident. You know I wouldn't intentionally smash her lamp."

Mom looked puzzled.

"Lamp? I don't know anything about a lamp."

Whoops. Wrong answer. Maybe Merrill hadn't snitched. Diane must have pulled off some minor miracle . . . maybe duct-taping his mouth? At any rate, whatever Mrs. Pelletier had called about had nothing to do with broken pottery.

The sick feeling, which had faded during the Barbie blasting, swept over me again. Foreboding.

"What did Mrs. Pelletier say?" I asked.

"Tell me about the lamp," Mom shot back.

"Well," I began, trying to think fast. Don't lie, said a little voice in my head. You know you will get caught, and then you'll be in worse trouble. So I tried a low-key approach that told the truth, the half truth, and nothing but the truth.

"We were in the guest room and I tripped over the edge of the bedspread. I bumped into the night table, a lamp tipped, and it broke. It was a total accident, Mom."

She shook her head, sighed, and pulled up a stool.

"And I suppose this happened while you were telephoning the Levesques?" she asked quietly.

Bingo. The moms knew. This was bad.

I pulled up a stool and waited. Mom decided to drop the Inquisition and get to it.

"Marie got a call this afternoon from Meredith Levesque," she said. "Meredith told her that some girls had made a prank call from the Pelletiers' number. Your name was specifically mentioned. She said the joke had something to do with a girl stranded at the movie theater? A maid who doesn't speak English? At any rate, Meredith ended up leaving her house and heading to the theater to find this kid. Luckily, her son telephoned her before she got there. *One* girl apparently had the good sense to call the Levesques and let them know it was a prank!"

"Oh my god!" I burst out. "The whole thing was *that girl's* idea!"

"Well, let me tell you," Mom burst back, "it was a *stupid* idea. To her credit, Meredith isn't particularly upset. She Googled the number to get the name on the phone account and called Marie just to let her know that some kids were using her phone inappropriately. But are you aware"—Mom looked meaningfully at me—"that Marie uses their home phone for her decorating business? *And* are you aware that Meredith and Drew Levesque are brand-new clients of Marie's? Let me tell you, Marie is ripped. This was very embarrassing for her."

"I thought you just said Mrs. Levesque wasn't too upset," I said.

"Meredith Levesque has impeccable manners," my mother replied. "She lives in a small town and understands that you handle things politely."

That hit me. Small town. Mess up in a small town and live with it forever. I wondered if this was a good time to bring up private school. Or moving.

"I don't know, Brett," Mom sighed, shaking her head. She

seemed deflated now, de-angered. "This is the last thing Marie needs right now. What were you thinking?"

What-were-you-thinking. Let-me-tell-you. Don't-speak-to-me-in-that-tone. Did someone give them a book in the maternity ward called *Really Annoying Things for Parents to Say*?

Then, just when I thought the conversation couldn't possibly get any worse, it did.

"You know, you're going to have to apologize," Mom said.

No. No no no no way. I was prepared to pack up, on the spot, and move to another town. I was willing to telephone every private school in Maine and request transfer applications. I would have even considered renouncing my U.S. citizenship and relocating to Singapore, or some other country on the farthest point of the planet away from Mescataqua. But apologize to the mother of the Hottest Boy in Maine, when all I really wanted to do was crawl under a rock and hide?

"You're kidding, right?" I said hopefully.

"I'm as serious as a heart attack," she replied.

Evil. My mother had become evil. Cruella de Vil, Cinderella's stepmother, and the witch queen from Snow White all rolled into one. Only that morning she had packed my snack of a Little Debbie Swiss Cake Roll, waved, and said, "I love you—have a great day!" when I'd headed out the door. What had happened to her while I was at school? Had aliens taken over her body?

"No."

It came out of me, simple as that. Just the one word.

"Brett, this is not negotiable." Mom was talking in her I-mean-business voice.

"Mom." I was talking in my pleading, I'm-on-the-verge-of-tears voice. "I'm really sorry I got involved in such a stupid joke. I'll call Diane's mom. But please don't make me call Mrs. Levesque."

"So write her a note," Mom said impatiently. "Why are you being so pigheaded?"

"Why are *you* making such a big deal about this?" I answered. "It's not like we were doing drugs or raiding the liquor cabinet. We played a dumb joke. Big deal!"

"You're absolutely right," Mom replied, putting her hands up in the I-surrender mode. "In the universe of big bad things kids do, this is minor. You weren't stealing cars or setting fires. But it *was* rude and you *do* need to offer a simple 'I'm sorry.' It's not the end of the world."

How could I possibly explain to her that it was? At least the world I inhabited, where Bob Levesque was the sun and the rest of the kids at Mescataqua Junior High School fought and bit and clawed for positions as minor planets in his orbit. My friends and I were tiny moons in the outermost regions of popularity, like Charon circling Pluto. Which isn't even a planet anymore.

Circling Pluto may not be very cool, but obscurity has its good points. People don't bother you if they don't notice you. And people like Bob Levesque for sure didn't notice me. Sure, in Girl Jock Universe I was a star. But step into the boy-girl world of going out, making out, weekend parties . . . and I was a dim bulb. They might be playing spin the bottle over at Bob's house, but I spent Saturday nights baking brownies with my grandmother.

I didn't want to think about what I would have to face at school the next day.

"You know, I think I'd like to go to my room, if that's okay," I said. "I don't want to talk about this anymore."

She pressed her lips together, nodded, breathed The Sigh, and I was dismissed. I scooped up my backpack and was just heading out the door when I remembered something.

"What did you mean by 'This is the last thing Marie needs right now'?" I asked.

Mom waved her hand as if the question were a mosquito. She didn't look at me. "Oh, nothing, really. We'll talk about it later. She's just under a lot of stress these days."

I wasn't the only one in the kitchen who had something she couldn't possibly explain.

dis·o·ri·ent·ed

After a half hour in my room with Good Charlotte (I played the refrain "Don't Want to Be Just Like You" six times at full volume), I was ready to make the first apology call. When I dialed, Mrs. Pelletier picked up.

She wasted no time in letting me know it would be a cold day in Quito before she forgave me or let Diane associate with me. (Quito is the capital of Ecuador, located smack on the equator.) I told her I was sorry, and I even offered to pay for the lamp, but that seemed to piss her off even more.

"You know, Brett," she said, her voice icy, "throwing money at a problem doesn't necessarily make it go away."

Frankly, I thought throwing money at a new lamp would go pretty far toward making the broken lamp go away. So when I finished apologizing, I asked to speak with Diane. That's when she announced The Ban.

"Diane is not allowed to use the phone for a week," Mrs.

Pelletier said. "And I don't know when she'll be allowed to see you." *Click*.

I was in no hurry to call Mrs. Levesque after that. So I wandered over to the Gnome Home to see what Bazooka Nonna was up to.

She was stacking the molded plastic chairs from the afternoon's entertainment in her garage and already knew the whole story. Apparently Mom had been over, filling her in while I was blowing out my eardrums in the bedroom. I told her about my call to Mrs. Pelletier. Nonna shook her head and settled into the top chair of the stack. Like she was sitting on a little throne.

"Well," she sighed, "as usual, Marie Pelletier is overreacting like a real rhymes-with-witch. You're just going to have to wait it out. But I'm proud of you for calling her. It's not easy to apologize, especially to someone who has trouble forgiving."

That was the thing about Nonna. She never let you get away with anything, but she always let you know she was on your side.

"I don't understand why she's *so* angry and why she won't let me pay for the lamp," I said.

"Well, she's got a lot on her mind right now," Nonna said.

"That's just what Mom said!" I burst out. "What are you guys talking about?"

Nonna looked at me, eyebrows raised.

"Has Diane told you about how her family's doing?" Nonna asked.

Now it was my turn to look puzzled. Diane and I talked all the time, but frankly, I couldn't recall hearing any important family news recently.

"What I'm going to say doesn't go beyond this . . . garage," Nonna continued, her eyes briefly scanning the mausoleum of old toys, bicycle parts, and cast-off windows that filled every corner of the building.

"It looks like Larry Pelletier is leaving Marie."

For a moment I thought I hadn't heard correctly. I felt disoriented, the way you feel when you walk into a quiet room and suddenly people jump out from behind the curtains shouting, "Surprise!"

Disoriented: *to lose one's sense of time, place, or identity.*

Mr. Pelletier leaving Mrs. Pelletier? After all the work they'd done on that house? After two kids? They were both *old* . . . at least in their forties, like my parents . . . what was the point? Nonna had to be wrong.

"No way," I replied. "Diane would have told me."

"Maybe she doesn't know yet," Nonna replied. "Marie told your mother this afternoon. Brett, you know I hate gossip. But I think knowing might help you understand why Diane's mother is overreacting."

I didn't know what to say. My head buzzed, and more than anything I needed to talk to Diane, right then. But we were banned. That's when I remembered Instant Messenger.

"Nonna, I think I need to get started on my homework," I said. She looked at me, surprised.

"Well, okay," she laughed. "I guess we're done with that subject. Or do you just want to get out of here?"

I bent over Nonna, seated on her plastic throne, wrapped my arms around her bird-bone shoulders, and squeezed. She smelled like fresh laundry detergent.

"Thank you," I whispered. For not hating me for calling the Levesques, I thought. For not keeping secrets from me. She patted the top of my head with her incredibly wrinkly hands.

"You know," she said, "you still haven't told me what you think of our Potato Bazooka."

bal·lis·tic

Diane didn't go online until that evening. At that point Dad was home too, and the three of us were in our usual spots in the kitchen: Dad sorting mail and getting interested in the evening paper, Mom doing something with dinner, me at the computer. I had pretended to do homework for more than an hour, Sockrgurl waiting impatiently for 2Di4 to sign on.

Just when I began to suspect that Mrs. Pelletier might have also imposed a computer ban, "hey!" appeared on the screen. Diane was on.

> **Sockrgurl:** whazzup?
>
> **2Di4:** mom's ballistic.

Ballistic: *moving like a projectile or rocket in flight.* Stratospherically angry.

> **Sockrgurl:** i thought merrill snitched
> but mom said mrs. I called?
>
> **2Di4:** yup. she's a client. mom's totally

embarrassed. made me drive w/her 2 l's. F2F apology.

Sockrgurl: OMG what happened?!?

2Di4: it was ok. as j a says, mrs. l is really really nice. i think she felt sorry 4 me 'cuz mom was way over the top, sucking up to the l's. etc. mrs. l invited mom to have a glass of wine & talk upholstery.

Sockrgurl: so?

2Di4: i hung w/bob while they had wine.

I stared at my screen. No way.

Sockrgurl: r u kidding?

2Di4: he's wicked cool. he had some friends over & we played foosball in the basement. they have a totally awesome house.

I was stunned. My best friend had just spent the afternoon with the hottest guy in Mescataqua, possibly in all of Maine. The worst, most embarrassing punishment in the world had somehow turned into a huge step up the social ladder.

Sockrgurl: wow. amazing.

2Di4: j a won't believe it.

I felt the back of my neck stiffen. Diane seemed to have forgotten that "j a" had caused all this trouble to begin with. Even if she, Diane, had just taken the miraculous step of having a conversation with the godlike Bob Levesque, entering his home and touching his foosball table, she was still banned from the phone and forbidden to see me. Her best friend.

> **Sockrgurl:** who sez we r talking 2 j a??
> **2Di4:** u rn't still blaming her r u?
> **Sockrgurl:** r u kidding? this was totally her idea! she called l & used my name! she got us in trouble! she's an idiot!
> **2Di4:** ok she shouldn't have used your name. but mrs. l is glad someone called so she didn't drive around looking 4 josephine.

I stared at the screen. Somehow, this "conversation" wasn't going right. Was 2Di4 taking "j a's" side? Just then she sent another message.

> **2Di4:** G2G.TTYL.

The message "2Di4 has signed off" popped up, and Diane disappeared into cyberspace. Nothing about her parents.

"Brett, dinner." My parents carried steaming plates to the kitchen table. Mom had made one of my favorites: meat loaf and mashed potatoes. I knew it was her way of making peace. Of getting us back to a normal, good place, where we hung out in the kitchen after school and talked about easy stuff, like sports or Nonna's latest inventions.

As I sat down at my place at the table, I caught Dad's eye. He winked at me and put one hand over mine.

" 'You may write me down in history / With your bitter, twisted lies. / You may trod me in the very dirt / But still, like dust, I'll rise,' " he said quietly. "Maya Angelou."

One of the weird things about having an English professor for a dad is that he quotes poetry at random moments. One of the cool things is that when you've screwed up, he quotes poetry instead of getting mad. Quoting Maya Angelou was Dad's way of letting me know he'd heard all about my great day. I winked back at him, then filled my mouth with meat and gravy.

"Mmmm. My favorite," I said, glancing at Mom. My way of making peace. If I had decided to keep the Cold War going, I would have taken two bites, pushed the plate away, and asked to be excused to do homework. But I'm too much of a chow hound to be a successful Cold Warrior, especially when the potatoes are garlic-mashed.

Anyone peering in the window would have seen a happy family having a perfectly ordinary evening together. But as Tuesday, October 16th, drew to a close, I knew it was going to take more than meat loaf to make things normal. And while I had a feeling Diane was looking forward to school the next day, I sure wasn't.

fea·si·ble

As I stared at my bedroom ceiling the night of October 16th, two questions kept a steady drumbeat in my head. First: What was the feasibility of hiding my identity at school the next morning? Could I slip on dark glasses and a hat every time I saw Bob Levesque?

Feasible: *capable of being done or carried out; likely.*

Second: How had the Pelletiers broken the news to Diane and Merrill that they were splitting? Was it feasible that Diane didn't know yet? Was it likely that she already knew and hadn't said a word to anyone?

Morning and October 17th finally came, and I stumbled to the bathroom. The big raccoon circles under my eyes, the direct result of no sleep, were the bad news. The good news: I wouldn't need a disguise at school after all, because no one would recognize me.

Not wanting to face Mom's inevitable "My goodness! Do you feel all right?" when she saw my eyes, I raced through a quick shower, packed my gym bag (we had a soccer game that afternoon), and grabbed a box of blueberry Pop-Tarts. I shouted goodbye toward my parents' bedroom as I headed out the door and walked to school.

Pop-Tarts are sort of okay toasted and totally gross untoasted, so after the third one I needed a drink, badly, to wash the saturated-fat gunk down my throat. I also needed to wipe off my shirt; it's hard to walk and eat breakfast at the same time. So I headed to the outdoor water fountain behind the main school building.

If you had asked me to list the Top Ten People Brett McCarthy Didn't Want to See at the Water Fountain, I couldn't have come up with anything nearly as bad as I actually encountered. Rounding the corner at a full run, I crashed into some tall guy's T-shirted back.

"Hey, watch it!" he exclaimed. There was something sickeningly familiar about the "Hey, watch it!"

Of course, it was Bob Levesque. Who else on the planet could possibly be standing at the back-lot water fountain— what I believed to be the least-frequented place in the entire school, except for maybe the custodian's supply closet in the basement? If I hadn't known it before, I sure knew it then: Brett McCarthy was the unluckiest piece of dead meat in Maine.

Bob took a step back. A semicircle of tall, cool guys, followers of the Greek God Levesque, stared at me. A sort of haze hung around their heads, and the place smelled. On the ground in front of them were discarded cigarette butts, and I realized, with the typical delayed reaction of an uncool kid who finally *gets* what the cool kids are up to, that this was where they came to smoke.

Then the kicker.

"Well, if it isn't Josephine," sneered a particularly annoying voice.

Jeanne Anne. She wasn't smoking (I'll give her that), but she was standing alongside Darcy Dodson, a.k.a. Darcy the Ditz to me and Diane. The meanest, skinniest member of the Mescataqua Junior High Cheerleading Squad, and one of Jeanne Anne's neighbors.

"Hey, Josephine. Slow down and have a smoke," said one of the Demigods. The others laughed.

"No way," said Darcy. "She's one of those super jocks. You know, protects her lungs, eats health food." I wondered if Darcy considered Pop-Tarts health food.

"Whatever," said another deity from the semicircle. "As long as you aren't a narc. You aren't going to tell anyone about our little . . . uh, meeting. Are you, Josephine?"

I shook my head. Speech was not a possibility. My teeth seemed permanently cemented shut by the pastry and blueberry goo.

Then the bell rang and the deities dispersed, dropping their cigarettes in the dirt and grinding them out with their heels. Jeanne Anne walked up to me.

"See you around. Josephine." She looked at Bob and raised

her eyebrows knowingly at the "Josephine" before sauntering off. Then it was Darcy's turn. She jabbed a red-lacquered fingernail into my chest and smirked.

"Next time try eating the food instead of wearing it." She and Jeanne Anne burst into hilarious giggles, then disappeared around the corner.

As soon as they were out of sight, I lunged for the water fountain. I must have sucked down a gallon before coming up for air—that's how long it took to clear my throat. When I lifted my head, I saw I wasn't alone.

Bob was still there. It was a little strange to see him without the usual crowd of adoring fans. He seemed serious, which, unbelievably, only made him look better.

"You're Brett McCarthy, right?" he asked quietly. I nodded.

"You know, Brett," he said, "my mother is a nice person. She doesn't deserve to have people play stupid jokes on her and waste her time. That was a real loser thing to do." Then Bob Levesque, God of Hotness, Loyal Son, turned and walked away without a backward glance.

Leaving me, Low-Life Insect, Deadest Meat on the Planet, wondering how I was ever going to make it through school that day.

As it turns out, I wouldn't have to.

un·prec·e·dent·ed

Here's the most important thing to know about junior high: Bad news travels fast and good news is a well-kept secret.

And at Mescataqua Junior High, really bad news, the juicy kind that ruins lives, travels at the speed of sound.

I don't know how she did it, but between four-thirty p.m., October 16th, and eight a.m. the following day, Jeanne Anne managed to torpedo my reputation. Granted, I had played a role in my own destruction. But the instant I saw her with Darcy the Ditz, I knew I was sunk. They had obviously walked to school together that morning, something Jeanne Anne would have arranged the night before. Which meant that before the sun had even set on October 16th, Jeanne Anne had told Darcy about the whole Levesque thing. And Darcy, no doubt, would have done a global message to everyone on her Way Popular Buddy List.

Okay, maybe not. But even paranoids have enemies. And as I headed into the building that morning, things looked bad.

For starters, no one was at The Junior. This was unprecedented.

Unprecedented: *new, having no example.*

We always waited by The Junior for each other, even if the bell had rung. For the first time, I walked into school alone.

That's when I saw it: the looks and nudges kids gave one another in the hall as I trudged in. I heard it in the whispers behind my back as I fumbled with my locker. And I felt it, like a kick to my gut, when I walked into first period and saw Diane seated near Jeanne Anne, their heads close together, talking.

When Jeanne Anne saw me, she straightened up, signaling Diane to be quiet. Not good.

"Hey, how's it goin'?" I said, plunking into the seat alongside Diane. She smiled. She looked like her normal, gorgeous self. Not like someone who had stayed up all night staring at the ceiling. Jeanne Anne, seated in front of us, looked straight ahead at the blackboard.

"Great," Diane said.

"I didn't see you out front," I continued.

Diane raised her eyebrows. "Well, I hear *you* were out back."

"Gee, I wonder where you heard *that*." I raised my voice just a bit. Jeanne Anne, back rigid, didn't turn.

"Some people are so boring, the only thing they can talk about is . . . other people," I continued. Jeanne Anne still faced forward.

"And some people are so *desperate*," I went on, "they'll even walk to school with losers, gossiping the whole time." That did it. She spun around.

"*Look* who's talking!" she practically shouted. "The overweight human sweatshirt! Who has nothing better to do than hang out with her garbage-collecting grandmother and math-team weirdos!"

The "overweight" alone didn't justify what followed, especially since I know it's not true. The fact is I'm big-boned, and fairly muscular for an eighth-grade girl. And the "math-team weirdo" bit? Well, it wouldn't be the first time Michael had taken heat for being Gifted and Talented. But "garbage-collecting?" My Nonna?

"You ugly cow," I said as my fist connected with her nose. Blood spurted.

Unprecedented. In the annals of Brett McCarthy screwups, a collection that seemed to be rapidly growing, this was a first. And in the history of Mescataqua Junior High, a fistfight between two girls was also unprecedented. Although it wasn't much of a fistfight. Jeanne Anne never hit back. She screamed for tissues while her nose bled all over Diane's language arts binder and the rest of the class chanted, "Cat fight! Cat fight!" Language arts teacher, who suddenly materialized from nowhere, thrust a box of Kleenex into some girl's hands, and ordered her to take Jeanne Anne to the nurse's office.

"You," he said, pointing a stubby index finger in my face. "Gather up your things. Let's go."

Our destination was the principal's office, where, following a long lecture about the Mescataqua Junior High School Zero Tolerance Policy on Violence, I was formally suspended. Three days starting today, no school. Which also meant no soccer, and we had two big games that week. As I waited for Dad to pick me up, my soccer coach, Mrs. LaVoie, came in and sat down beside me. Like I said, bad news travels fast.

"Brett, I want to say I'm surprised, but I'm not," she said gently. "I'm shocked. Dumbfounded. This is completely uncharacteristic. Is there something going on that you want to talk about?"

In addition to coaching soccer, Mrs. LaVoie teaches language arts at our school. She was my sixth-grade L.A. teacher, and she and I are each other's biggest fans. Not only are we really into soccer, but she gets my word thing and speaks to me like I'm an intelligent human being. Mom and Dad love her because she called a special meeting with them to discuss my "talent with language." She always asks me if I've been doing any writing, which makes me feel guilty, because I'm not. But it also makes me feel good that she believes in me.

So there I was, sitting in the principal's office, shattering her illusions that I was anything special. I'd like to say I was cool. I'd like to say I took my punishment bravely, unremorsefully, if there is such a word.

Instead, I burst into tears. I blubbered. By the time Dad got there, I had stopped crying, but my raccoon-circled eyes were now puffy and red as well. Dad spent some time in the hall talking with Mrs. LaVoie before leading me out, arm across my shoulders.

"It'll be okay, Brett," he said when we got in the car. "Remember: 'It matters not how strait the gate, / How charged with punishments the scroll, / I am the master of my fate: / I am the captain of my soul.' William Ernest Henley." I saw him attempt a smile. "In other words, honey, we'll work this out. Things can't get any worse."

But they did.

awk·ward

Suspension, if you want my opinion, is ridiculous. First, you take the worst kids in the school system. They do something awful, like smoke dope. Call in a bomb scare. Hit Jeanne Anne. Then you kick them out for days, with zero supervision. Most of these kids have working parents who aren't home during school hours. So these troublemakers have the run of the town, time on their hands, and nobody watching.

Is it really true that school superintendents, who make up these rules, have PhDs?

There was no sign of Mom and Nonna by the time we arrived. This put Dad in an awkward position, forcing him to choose between staying home with his violent daughter or hurrying off to teach his morning class.

Awkward: *showing lack of expertness; lacking social grace and assurance.*

More and more, Lecturing Brett ended up on Mom's to-do

list. It's funny: Dad can lecture to an auditorium full of students, but spend fifteen minutes asking his teenage daughter how she managed to get herself thrown out of school? No way.

Don't get me wrong. Dad's a great guy, in a flaky, professor-like way. But it seemed like ever since I'd started wearing a bra, he'd forgotten how to talk to me. Unless it was about a poem.

So after assuring him that I really hadn't become a juvenile delinquent, and that if it weren't for Jeanne Anne I would still be an upstanding honors student with an unblemished record, he decided to go to work.

"You won't burn the house down while I'm gone, right?" he joked as he headed out the door. At least I think he was joking. He stuck a note on the fridge for Mom, saying he'd be home early and would she please call him before speaking to me.

I figured I had two options: Sit there and wait for Mom and The Lecture of a Lifetime, or hide at the Gnome Home until dinner.

I decided to delay the inevitable.

Nonna's house was unlocked and smelled like warm chocolate. I found a pan of just-baked brownies taking up space on her cluttered kitchen table, along with loose-leaf notebook pages covered with pencil drawings.

I carved a hunk of brownie from the pan, poured a glass of milk, and sat. As I chewed (double fudge with raspberry chips), I leafed through the drawings. Someone had sketched a candle. Little squares arranged in a circle. Then I saw something familiar.

"It's Spruce Island light," I said, so surprised that I announced it to the empty room. The old lighthouse—and I'm talking really old, like, built when Thomas Jefferson was president—on Nonna's island.

For as long as I can remember, one of Nonna's defining maverick qualities has been her desire to restore Spruce Island light. She'd tried to have it added to some registry of historic places. Tried to have the Coast Guard recommission it. Tried to convince the Maine Maritime Academy in Castine that rebuilding a decrepit lighthouse would be a wonderful project for future sailors. But the lighthouse remained as it always had: a shell of a stone tower with a rusty catwalk on top, surrounded by weeds, with hidden caches of old nails and broken glass.

"If she ever pulls this off, it will be a Pyrrhic victory indeed," Dad once said. I'd asked him what the heck *that* meant, and he explained that Pyrrhus was an ancient king of Epirus who defeated the Roman army only after a great many of his soldiers had died. So, Dad said, a "Pyrrhic victory" is won at excessive cost. In other words, it would cost Nonna a bundle to get the light fixed.

Do other kids' dads talk like this?

As I sifted through the papers, I heard a car door slam. Through the kitchen window I saw Mom and Nonna emerging from the car. Uh-oh, I thought. Time to retreat. I ducked into the living room, crouching behind the sofa as they walked in. Not very dignified, but I could see them if I peeked around the corner.

Mom carried grocery bags and began unloading them onto the counters. Nonna settled into a kitchen chair. That's when I realized I'd left my half-finished glass of milk on the table. And the pan with one enormously missing brownie.

"You know, Eileen," Mom said, "maybe it is just allergies, or some sort of infection. But the MRI will rule out anything bad, and we won't have to worry."

"He's overreacting," Nonna said. "This is why health care in this country is so expensive. All these ridiculous tests for nothing." I saw Nonna pick up my milk glass and frown.

"Well," Mom said briskly, "better safe than sorry. I should go home and check the answering machine. The hospital may have called to let us know when we can come in." Mom left. I watched Nonna place the milk glass back on the table.

"Okay," she said, in a voice clearly intended to carry into the next room. "I know only one person who cuts brownies from the middle of the pan. Come out and explain why you're home from school." Awkwardly, I crawled on all fours from behind the sofa.

"Thanks for not giving me away," I said.

Nonna frowned. "How long have you been here?"

"Five minutes. Dad brought me home because you and Mom were out. Where were you guys?"

"Are you sick?" Nonna continued.

"No. Suspended."

"Suspended!" she repeated. "What for?"

"I hit someone," I said. "Nonna, what were you and Mom talking about?"

"Your mother doesn't know, does she?" Nonna said, narrowing her eyes. "Brett. You know I don't like you to keep secrets from your mother."

"It's not a secret," I sighed, flopping into the kitchen chair. "I just haven't told her. Yet." I picked up one of the loose-leaf sheets. "Speaking of secrets, what is this?"

Nonna passed her hand over her eyes. She seemed tired. "Honey, stick to the topic."

Just then the car pulled into the driveway again. The Return of Mom.

"Oh, no," I exclaimed, jumping up and backing into the living room. "Nonna, I really don't want to deal with Mom right now." I looked pleadingly into Nonna's eyes. She shook her head again but waved me toward the sofa.

"Tonight," she said as Mom's footsteps crunched along the walkway gravel. "You tell her tonight." The door opened.

"Hey. They can see us right now." Mom made this announcement as she leaned into the kitchen.

"Okay," said Nonna, pulling herself up from her chair.

"Let's do it." From my hiding place I could see Mom glance toward the cluttered table, the brownie pan. She smiled.

"I can see you haven't lost your appetite," she said cheerfully, holding the door open for Nonna.

"Don't be so sure," Nonna said.

in·fer·no

So with Dad at work, Nonna and Mom off on some mysterious medical mission, and the rest of the world in school, I did what comes naturally when my stress meter hits code red. I polished off another brownie, then went home and crawled into bed. I don't know how long I slept before the sound of a ringing doorbell dragged me from oblivion and back to the reality of my incredibly suckulous life.

I stumbled downstairs to the front door wrapped in my comforter, hair standing stiff, troll-like. I tend to wake up badly.

It was Michael.

"Oh, hey," I said. "Since when do you ring?" I headed to the kitchen, comforter and Michael trailing.

"The door was locked. You've been sleeping?" he asked, surprised. We sat on opposite ends of the kitchen window seat. The sun was doing its late-day, mid-autumn slant thing, shining horizontally and into my eyes through the big windows.

My soccer team was probably playing at that very moment. Mom and Nonna still hadn't returned.

"So. Tell me. How bad is it?" I asked him. "And I don't mean my hair."

"Scale of one to ten?" he asked.

"With one being 'life as usual' and ten being 'transfer to another school,' " I replied. Michael looked thoughtful.

"Depends," he said.

"On?"

"Whether or not you think Jeanne Anne deserves a broken nose," he said.

"No!" I groaned. "Is it broken? Absolutely?"

"Rumor has it," he said.

"Ten!" I wailed, burying my face in the comforter.

"Nah," Michael said. "Three. Okay, four, since we had to sit through a Zero Tolerance for Violence assembly. But you know, Brett, to some people you're a hero."

"Yeah?" I said, sarcastically. "Who?" Not Bob Levesque, I thought. Not anyone from the back-lot water fountain gang.

"Well," Michael said, "Kit. Your entire soccer team. All the kids Jeanne Anne has been mean to, which is most of the eighth grade. Me." The "me" came out sort of squeaky, like it was hard for him to say.

"Well, thanks for your undying loyalty. But I'm still hosed," I said. "Kit will be mad she didn't punch Jeanne Anne herself. My soccer team will be mad because I'm missing two important games. And you . . ." I trailed off.

"Too uncool to count?" Michael said.

"I'm sorry, I'm sorry," I said, instantly regretful. "That's *not* what I meant. I don't know what I mean. I'm really messed up, okay? I've gone from Model Scholar Athlete to Juvenile Delinquent in forty-eight hours, and it's a little disorienting."

Michael is probably the only kid I know who doesn't flinch or blink vacantly when I use a word like "disorienting."

There was a long silence before either of us spoke again.

"Why do you care so much what the popular kids think?" he finally said.

"I don't," I said instantly.

"Yeah, right," he replied. "Why else are you prank-calling Bob Levesque's mother? Why else would you get so mad at Jeanne Anne that you'd clock her? I mean, do you actually care what she thinks, or are you just pissed that she's moving into the popular circle?"

"Wait a minute," I said. "First of all, the Levesque thing was not my idea. Second, Jeanne Anne is *un*popular pond scum. No offense meant, but maybe from a high honors math team perspective, a loser like Jeanne Anne seems cool, but trust me, she's not."

"You are in such denial," he sighed. He heaved his backpack, stuffed tight with books, onto the window seat. No matter how much—or how little—homework we have, Michael hauls a library home each night. He pulled out a thin notebook, flipped through it, then slapped it open in my lap.

"Let me show you something I developed during Fifth Period."

Fifth Period, commonly known as the Gifted and Talented Hour, is when about a dozen or so of the Über Students, like Michael, are siphoned off from the rest of the herd for "special work." You can practically hear their brains pulsating from behind closed doors as they read impossibly difficult books, fold origami, and design engines that run on vegetable oil from the cafeteria's fryolator.

"I'm really not in the mood to admire your homework," I groaned. Michael continued, undeterred.

"Dante Alighieri was a thirteenth-century Italian writer who wrote a poem about Hell," said Michael. "He imagined that Hell is divided into descending rings, with criminals suffering increasingly worse tortures the lower you went. He called it *The Inferno*."

Inferno: *a place that resembles Hell; intense heat.*

"Sounds lovely," I remarked.

"It was incredible," Michael said enthusiastically. "He worked out this whole hierarchy of evil and punishment, and then, to make things interesting, he told us who you'd find there. I mean, he named names. Popes. Rich men. Famous people. They thought they were golden, but Dante assigned them to Hell.

"Anyway, for one of my Fifth Period projects I thought it would be cool to compare the social hierarchy at Mescataqua to Dante's Inferno."

"Meaning you think we're all going to Hell?" I asked.

"Meaning *we're in* Hell," Michael said. "At least those of us obsessed with popularity."

I stared at the open notebook. Michael had drawn two stacks of rings. On the left Dante's Inferno, where he'd sketched little pearly gates and angels at the top and a nasty flame pit on the bottom. In between was Dante's order of evil from one through nine: Limbo, the Lustful, the Gluttonous, the Avaricious, the Wrathful, the Heretics, the Violent, the Frauds, and the Traitors. On the right he'd drawn the Mescataqua version: Undecided, Flirts and Hos, People Who Eat/Take More Than Their Share, the Greedy, the Perpetually Pissed Off, the Wishy-Washy, the Violent, the Backstabbers/Gossipers/Social Climbers, and the Traitors.

Dante's Inferno was just labeled rings, but Mescataqua's had people's names.

"Hey, you're not in it!" I said, my eyes scanning the diagram. "No fair."

"Yeah, but I *wrote* it. . . ."

"I see . . . so that makes you . . . Dante?"

Michael grinned.

"You move people around," I commented, noticing an erasure. "You had Kit in the Eat More Than Their Share ring, then moved her down to Greedy."

"Did you see what she did to that pizza we had on the half day?" he exclaimed. "I got one slice; she took *five*. She's beyond hungry. She's, like, a predator."

He'd placed Jeanne Anne, appropriately enough, in Ring Eight with the Backstabbers. Darcy was penciled in with Flirts and Hos, way too high as far as I was concerned. Brett McCarthy was . . . Undecided?

"Why am I Undecided?" I asked, looking up.

"I think I know you too well to generalize," he said. "I put you there because . . . well, where do *you* think you belong?"

"Given today?" I replied. "Holding steady in the lower reaches of Ring Seven. The Violent."

Then I noticed something that surprised me. Michael had originally stuck Diane in Ring Six, the Wishy-Washy, but crossed out her name and placed her in Ring Eight. He'd written "Social Climbers" next to her name.

"Why'd you demote Diane?" I asked.

"Because she's trying to move into the popular group," Michael said matter-of-factly.

"How so?"

"How about . . . trying out for cheerleading after school today."

I thought I hadn't heard him correctly.

"Diane tried out for cheerleading?" My voice sounded stupid in my ears.

"I almost didn't recognize her," Michael continued. "She had her hair pulled back tight, and it kind of stretched her eyes sideways. But there she was, with Darcy and the whole gang from the Second Ring."

My brain froze, then moved in slow motion as I processed

this information. No one just tried out for cheerleading. You signed up in advance, practiced routines . . . usually with other girls. Other cheerleaders.

"Wow," Michael said. He was staring at me. "You didn't know. I figured you knew. I mean, you two are so tight."

I shook my head. The Vocab Ace Queen of Denial was at a loss for words.

"Wow," Michael repeated.

"Stop saying 'wow,' " I snapped. I was suddenly really sick of Michael.

"Okay, well, maybe I should . . . head home," he said, gently pulling the notebook from my lap.

"Whatever," I said. A totally unfriendly response, especially since he was the only person from school who had bothered to check in with me that afternoon. But I'm not particularly nice when I feel stupid and betrayed.

"I'll see you around," he said, shouldering his filled-to-capacity backpack and heading out the kitchen door. He practically ran over Mom, who was just walking in.

"Hello, Michael!" she said brightly. "Just leaving?" He muttered something approaching hi-yup-gotta-go, and disappeared. Mom tossed her keys and purse on the kitchen counter, unbuttoned her jacket, and flopped onto the space of window seat just vacated by Michael. She closed her eyes briefly, then smiled.

"How was your day?" she said. "I hope it was better than mine."

ob·tuse

Here's the thing about parents: Just when you think you've got them totally figured out, they surprise you.

I would have bet my cleats that Mom's Lecture of a Lifetime would be full of the usual Really Annoying Things Parents Say. What-Were-You-Thinking. I'm-So-Disappointed-in-You. How-Many-Times-Do-I-Have-to-Tell-You. I could go on, but it's too annoying even to list them.

Then she went and blew my assumptions out of the water.

For starters, she didn't lecture me. First she telephoned Dad (rather than launch into the sad story of my disastrous day, I directed her to Dad's fridge note). They talked for a long time. After she hung up, she returned to the window seat and got right to the point. No Inquisition, no annoying lead-in.

"Let me make sure I've got this straight," she said quietly. "You punched Jeanne Anne because she made fun of your grandmother?"

I nodded and waited for the storm. Instead, Mom wrapped

her arms tight around me and held on for probably a whole minute. When she let go, I could swear she looked teary.

"Good for you," she said. "Don't you let anyone make fun of Nonna. Ever."

I stared at her in amazement.

"Whoa," I said. "Whatever happened to 'Sticks and Stones Can Break My Bones'? You'd better watch it, Mom, or someone is going to make you attend a Zero Tolerance for Violence assembly. Trust me; they're no fun."

She laughed, wiping her eyes. What's up? I thought. She's crying.

"Tell you what," she said. "Daddy's coming home early. I'm going to get started on dinner. Why don't you head over to Nonna's and ask her to join us tonight?"

I looked at her suspiciously.

"No lecture?" I asked.

"Nope."

"You aren't angry?"

She paused.

"I don't know what I am," she said. "I'm in a place so far beyond angry that I can't quite recognize it. Call it 'numb.' At any rate, enjoy it now, because I'll have plenty of time to get mad at you over the next few days. Now get going. Tell her I'm making pasta. She loves pasta."

Obtuse. Means *lacking sharpness or quickness of sensibility*. Also means *stupid*. *Clueless*.

Because I finally got it. The pasta made it all clear. Here I was, suspended and temporarily banned from soccer, which in my definition is a Big Bad Deal, but all Mom could think about was . . . noodles. Nonna's favorite food.

There had been a zillion signs. Ever since Nonna had returned from Spruce Island. But I had been too obtuse to notice until now.

Something was wrong with my grandmother, and Mom was worried sick.

an·tip·a·thy

Nonna was busy at the stove. She promptly turned down the invitation to pasta.

"I've got Beady coming over tonight," she said. "Tell your mother thanks anyway."

I settled into a kitchen chair. Nonna had replaced the clutter on the table with two place settings. The room smelled like something burning. Despite my antipathy for Mr. Beady, I felt sorry for him. Nonna was a world-renowned bad cook. Unless she was cooking with chocolate. It was one of her odd little defining qualities. Her chocolate desserts were amazing, but everything else she cooked . . . yuck.

Antipathy: *dislike engendering feelings of extreme annoyance.*

"So," she said as she scraped the pan, "did you finally tell her?"

"Yup," I replied.

"And how did it go?" she asked.

"She seemed a little preoccupied," I said.

Nonna shut off the burner and turned.

"Her daughter gets suspended from school and she's preoccupied? That doesn't sound like your mother."

"Well, I think she's worried about you," I said.

Nonna frowned. "What did she tell you?" she asked.

"Nothing. But even someone as clueless as me can tell something's up. Why were you guys at the doctor's today?"

Nonna sighed and pulled up an adjacent kitchen chair.

"I've never seen such overreaction," she said. "You know, I hate to surprise you all, but I'm an old lady! These wrinkles are real! And I think I overdid it at the island this summer. I felt tired, came back early, and next thing I know, your mother is dragging me to the doctor because she doesn't like my 'color.' My color! 'Have you ever seen a suntan before?' I asked her. Then Dr. Fischer starts asking me all these questions, and gets all wide-eyed when I tell him I think I caught a bit of brown-tail moth. I've been itchy for weeks, and the cortisone cream isn't helping. Next thing you know, he's sending me for bloodwork and an MRI!"

"MRI?" I asked.

"Magnetic resonance imaging," she said. "Takes a picture of your organs. He wanted to peek at my pancreas."

"What's a pancreas?" I asked.

"As far as I'm concerned, it's an expensive distraction!"

Nonna said, returning to her smoking pan. "I'm having an allergic reaction to something, and these doctors want to order up unnecessary tests! Meanwhile, I'm itchy and irritable and your mother is so worried that she's not taking care of business. Which means reprimanding you for hitting someone at school!"

"Maybe I should send Dr. Fischer a thank-you note?" This conversation was making me feel much better. Nonna sure wasn't acting sick.

"You're not getting off that easy," she said. "Since your mother is too 'preoccupied' to deal with you, I'll hand down the sentence. And you know how I feel about violence."

"I know," I said.

"There's no excuse for hitting someone, Brett."

"Hmmm," I said. I wished, really wished, that I saw it her way. But I'm not as good a person as my grandmother.

"I'd say a little community service is in order. How long are you suspended?"

"The rest of the week."

"That's just enough time to help me sort out the entire garage and get organized for my sale. We'll hold it this weekend, you'll be in charge, and we'll donate all the proceeds to the Domestic Violence Prevention Center."

I groaned. Not that I had anything against the Domestic Violence Prevention Center. But Nonna's garage was a mess.

Dusty, rusty, moldy junk was stacked floor to ceiling. I didn't want to touch it.

Before I could think of a way to wriggle out of my sentence, Mr. Beady tapped on the door.

"Come in, Beady!" Nonna said. "I'm running a little late."

Mr. Beady carried a paper bag. I could see the top of a wine bottle and a bag of corn chips poking from the top. He raised his eyebrows when he saw me.

"Well, if it isn't the local boxin' champ!" He grinned. "How's it goin', *sluggah*?"

Mr. Beady is not a native Mainer. He's "from away." Born in Connecticut, actually. And when he tries to imitate a Maine accent, it's really annoying.

"How'd you hear?" I asked him.

"Oh, it's all the talk of the grocery *stow-ah*," he said. "Sorry, Eileen. I forgot salsa," he added to Nonna.

"Look in the fridge," she replied.

"Miss Brett, will you be joinin' us tonight for . . ." Mr. Beady peered into Nonna's pan. "Blackened *gah-lick*?"

"No thanks," I said, getting up. "Mom's serving edible food at home."

"Ah, we will have to check in another time for tales of your ignominious day." He chuckled. Ignominious. I had no clue what that meant. When he wasn't imitating a lobsterman, Mr. Beady sounded like a professor. He was being even more annoying than usual this evening.

"Good night, sweetie," Nonna said, blowing a kiss in my direction. "Come by in the morning, and we'll get started." I nodded, heading out. It was dark already, and as I pulled the door shut against the warm glow of the kitchen light, I heard Nonna speak.

"Beady, what does a pancreas do?"

re·con·sti·tute

Frugality is practically a religion in Maine. Even those who can afford full price at the mall brag that they bought it for peanuts at Goodwill. And yard sales . . . the Promised Land of the Thrifty . . . are a pretty big deal and fairly competitive.

Even by Maine standards Nonna's Super-Sized was wildly popular. An annual Mescataqua event, actually. More like a wacky block party, or a science fair on steroids, than a garage sale.

For starters, she didn't sell anything useful. The pros always stayed away. That's because they knew they wouldn't find a single item that anyone in their right mind would want. No treasures or bargains, no practically new bicycles, no vases, bookcases, or ski boots. Still, most of Mescataqua came.

That's because Nonna specialized in what she called "reconstituted" items. My dad says when he was a boy, "reconstituted" orange juice was a big thing.

Reconstitute: *to restore to a former condition by adding water*. Like powdered milk.

With Nonna's items water played a minor role. But duct tape was key. Superglue. Nails, screws, soldering equipment. Anything it took to stick egg cartons onto wooden dowels, or join lengths of rusty pipe, or attach bedsprings to the bottoms of old boots. A little tape here, a little hinge there, and presto! A Ping-Pong catapult. Or pogo boots. Or a hamster hotel. Reconstituted from promising pieces of cast-off stuff she'd collected all year, and irresistible to your average child.

I loved the annual Super-Sized. Mr. Beady, Michael, and I would stay up late the night before, hard at it in the garage, arguing over things like why the Teddy Bear Carousel powered by the NordicTrack ski machine flywheel kept getting stuck. Diane, who always worked it with us, would help with the bake-sale component. She was hopeless at construction (she couldn't even *unwind* duct tape, let alone attach it to anything), so she always ended up in the kitchen, where she and Nonna turned out pan after pan of fudge brownies and choco-coconut dream bars.

Diane would also make her signature treat: madeleines, little French cakes baked in a specially molded pan. Nonna loved them but, true to form, was hopeless at making them. That's because madeleines don't contain one bit of chocolate, and Nonna could work her magic only if chocolate was involved. Diane, however, was a madeleine whiz.

On Super Sized mornings my parents would appear with hot chocolate, coffee, and Dunkin' Donuts. They never really got involved in the Super-Sized. Just spectated from afar. I think they appreciated that it was one of Nonna's special things.

But not this year. You'd think they were flies on sticky paper, the way they hung around. They'd shut the whole operation down early the night before, just when Michael and I were trying to put the final touches on the Ped-o-Sled (an old Flexible Flyer that we'd rigged up with fat tires, a seat, and pedals, perfect for pedaling over a snow-covered frozen lake).

"Let's wrap it up," Mom had said. "Nonna needs a good night's sleep."

There was an edge to her voice, and I got the impression that she didn't approve of the Super-Sized this year. She kept making comments to Dad about "overdoing it" and "not necessary." I could tell she was getting on Nonna's nerves.

When I arrived at the Gnome Home kitchen the morning of the sale, Nonna was slicing brownies into Super Sizes and wrapping them in plastic.

"There you are," she said. "Another minute and I was going to eat that last Boston kreme myself." She nodded toward a pink-and-yellow donut box on the table. I am mad for Boston kreme donuts. I flopped into a kitchen chair and helped myself.

"Is Michael here yet?" I asked.

"He and Beady are finishing up your Ped-o thing in the garage," she said. "It's hard to get it to move on the grass, but they think it'll work fine on ice or snow."

"Awesome," I said, taking a huge bite. The pastry-chocolate-custard combo was heavenly.

"You know, I've been trying to figure out what's different this year, and it finally occurred to me last night," said Nonna. "Diane hasn't come by to help. I can scarcely remember a Super-Sized without her."

"Umm," I replied, filling my mouth with donut.

"What's she up to these days?"

"No clue." I shrugged. "Her mother won't let her talk to me, and I've been kicked out of school, remember?" The truth, the half truth, and nothing but . . . the half truth? I could imagine Michael's expression if he heard this exchange.

"Well, I miss her," said Nonna. "I needed her in the kitchen last night. Speaking of which, start slicing dream bars. And make 'em huge."

The weather was perfect, and cars by the dozen started cruising up the driveway or parking along the side of the road earlier than we'd expected. Like I said, the Super-Sized was an annual Mescataqua event.

We all had our "positions." Nonna worked the bake-sale table, making a point of telling everyone that there was no charge for the goodies but contributions to the Domestic Violence Prevention Center could go in the glass mayonnaise jar. Two of the Kathies (who turned out to be volunteers at the Domestic Violence Prevention Center . . . go figure) helped people carry stuff to their cars. Michael and Mr. Beady were out back, blasting the bazooka. They'd put together "Build Your Own Bazooka" kits, complete with PVC pipe and instructions, and were trying to drum up business with exciting demonstrations. From the squeals and applause I heard, I could tell it was a big hit. But I didn't actually see anything. I'd gotten stuck at the Ping-Pong catapult table.

Ping-Pong balls really get on my nerves. I don't know, there's something about that irritating little sound they make when they bounce that crawls right up my spine. Stationing me at the catapult table, which turned out to be a seven-year-old-boy magnet, was torture.

To amuse myself I started firing balls at little kids. Families would stroll past my table, and I'd take aim at an unsuspecting childish leg and—*ping!*—bounce a ball off someone's socks at ten feet. Ironically, they all thought it was a big game and would come running over for more. Great.

I was squaring off with a pretty aggressive five-year-old (he'd already nailed me twice between the eyes) when I heard a familiar voice.

"Wow, that sure looks like fun. Maybe Brett can let you boys give it a try."

It was Mr. Pelletier. Merrill was with him, and another little boy I didn't recognize. My eyes darted, looking for Diane, but I didn't see her.

"So what do you call this?" Mr. Pelletier said cheerfully. Heartily, like someone who's trying to convince himself . . . and others . . . that he's having a good time.

"It's a Ping-Pong catapult," I answered, looking at Merrill and the boy. "Want to give it a try?"

The Merrill I used to know and despise would have knocked me over for a turn with the catapults. This sort of semiviolent plaything was right up his hyperactive alley. When he wasn't zoned out in front of the television, Merrill was whacking, bashing, tossing . . . you get the picture.

Not this Merrill. He stared down at the Velcro closures on his dusty Spider-Man sneakers and shrugged at my invitation. His companion, a slightly smaller blond boy with large, owl-eye glasses, did no better. He looked nervously at the catapults, biting his lower lip. He didn't seem at all like the usual juvenile delinquents Merrill associated with. Then a fourth person arrived on the scene and made everything clear.

"Hey, honey, what do we have here?"

A bird of paradise seated in an osprey's nest would have looked less incongruous at the Super-Sized than the woman who asked this question.

In Maine, where one is most likely to find a woman who can dismantle, clean, and reassemble a chain saw, this small, highly blond female person was clearly "from away."

Her "Hey, honey" placed her below the Mason-Dixon line. Her full-facial makeup glowed slightly orange, and her shiny, smooth coif was pulled back with a black velvet bow. She wore a fuzzy white sweater (*she* obviously had no intention of hauling rusty pipes back to her car), stretchy black slacks, and black leather boots with sharp heels that made little holes in the lawn. She placed one hand gently on the blond boy's shoulder and slid a slim, fuzzy arm around Mr. Pelletier's waist. It was not a sisterly embrace.

Holy crow, I thought. Mr. Pelletier's got a girlfriend.

Before I could fully absorb this information, Nonna arrived and blew me away entirely.

"Well, hello. We meet again," Nonna said. She was talking to the girlfriend, whose enormous, heavily mascaraed eyes widened in surprise.

"Mrs. McCarthy! Whatever are you doing here?"

"Well, I live here. We do this sale every year. I see you've met my granddaughter, Brett." Girlfriend locked her gaze on me.

"We haven't been properly introduced yet," she said. "Hello, Brett. I'm Pamela Warren. And this here's my son, Brock. And my friend, Larry Pelletier, and his little boy, Merrill."

"Actually, we know the Pelletiers," Nonna said. "Brett and Diane are practically sisters. Where is she today, Larry? I can't remember her ever missing a garage sale."

Mr. Pelletier grinned nervously and hesitated. I could see he wasn't sure what to say.

I could have answered for him. Diane wouldn't have been caught dead walking around and smiling at neighbors who would stare at Pamela Warren and whisper, "Who's that?"

Merrill confirmed this.

"She didn't want to come with us," he said softly. Un-Merrill-like.

"Oh, that's too bad," said Nonna soothingly. She directed her comment to Merrill. "You tell her we missed her, okay? Tell her we saved a Super-Sized brownie just for her."

Merrill stared miserably back at Nonna. His lower lip quivered. His big brown eyes glazed over with tears.

"I don't think she'll come," he whispered. "Can I bring it to her?"

This was blowing my mind. Merrill, the Dark Lord. The child most likely to have Damien's 666 tattooed on his scalp. Trying to do something nice for his sister? Unbelievable.

"Of course!" Nonna said. "And I'll get some for you and Brock too. Be right back." She hurried off to the bake-sale table, leaving me with Mr. Pelletier, the boys, and Southern Belle Barbie.

"Oh, isn't she just *precious*!" cooed Pamela Warren. "I tell you," she said to me, "I've only recently met your grandmother, but I absolutely love her. Look at her. And you know she doesn't feel well! But does she let that stop her? No, not her. I tell you, I *admire* her."

"How do you know my Nonna?" I asked, stupefied. How would you know she doesn't feel well? I wanted to ask.

"We met the other day at the hospital," she said. "I'm a hospice volunteer. We wanted to let your grandmother know what we're all about, what options are available to her. When she's ready." Pamela Warren smiled knowingly at me. My stomach did a one-eighty. Ready for what?

Nonna came back with the treats. They really were huge. One brownie looked almost as big as Brock's head.

"Now, why don't you take these around back and go see the bazooka blasting?" Nonna told them. "I think they're firing off old sneakers stuffed with styrofoam peanuts."

"'Bye!" said Pamela Warren gaily. "Mrs. McCarthy, you take care now. Don't overdo. I can see what you're like!" Nonna waved them on but said nothing. She pursed her lips tightly, ignoring my pointed stare.

"Later," Nonna said, not meeting my eyes. "Right now we have the sale to think about. But we'll discuss this later."

She headed over to the driveway, where more cars had just pulled in, and greeted the eager families who piled out. The Pelletier-Warrens were walking toward the bazookas. Brock had already unwrapped his brownie and was polishing it off in super-sized bites. Merrill held his treats to his chest and walked with his head down, kicking little dry scuffs of dirt along the way.

That's when I surprised myself. I grabbed two of the smaller catapults and a half dozen Ping-Pong balls off the table, stuffed them into a plastic shopping bag, and sprinted after Merrill.

"Here," I said, thrusting the bag into his hands when I

caught up with him. "You guys can shoot these at each other when you get home." Merrill peeked inside. His head shot up and he grinned at me. A flash of the old destructive Merrill. "Thanks!" he said, and bounded off toward the bazookas, his dad, and his own redefined life.

neu·tral

"He's got nerve. I'll say that much for him."

Mom, Dad, and I were breaking down the last remnants of the garage sale. As usual, the Super-Sized had been a smashing success. We'd unloaded everything—even the Ped-o-Sled—and made more than $400 for the Domestic Violence Prevention Center. Michael and Mr. Beady had sold five Build Your Own Bazooka kits, and the Gnome Home garage was completely clean. Not a rusty pipe or moldy tire in sight.

Nonna had gone inside for a nap. She was exhausted. She didn't even have the energy to argue with Mr. Beady, who had insisted on scrubbing the brownie pans stacked in the sink. Nonna hated the way Mr. Beady only half washed dishes. He was in there right now, and I couldn't believe she was able to sleep over all his clattering.

I had been waiting for someone to bring up the Mr. Pelletier thing. It was like an eight-hundred-pound gorilla in the living room: Everyone knew it was there, but no one wanted to mention it. I knew if it had been just Nonna and me, there'd be plenty to say. Instead, my parents were doing their usual job "talking" to me without really telling me anything.

"So," I'd finally said, "did you check out Mr. Pelletier's girlfriend?" I let that one hang in the air for a few seconds.

That's when Dad made the comment about nerve. Mom frowned at him and shook her head slightly, sending him one of those telepathic parental signals I supposedly didn't notice.

"What makes you think she was a girlfriend?" Mom asked neutrally. "Maybe she was just a friend."

Neutral: *neither one thing nor the other; indifferent, disengaged.*

"The way she had her hands all over him kind of screamed 'girlfriend' at me," I commented, equally neutral. "She was also really dressed up, like it was a date or something. You know, the fuzzy sweater and the high-heeled boots? The average mom at a garage sale usually isn't stylin' like that."

"She aerated Nonna's lawn for us," Dad said matter-of-factly. "You know, those stiletto boots? I'm thinking about buying a pair for you, hon." He winked at Mom.

"Yeah, you know, Mom, you could also use some fuzzy sweaters," I said.

"Oh, I don't know," Dad said. "Fiber artists don't do fuzzy,

Brett. Your mom's more the Wearable Art crowd. I like her handmade quilted vests."

"She could be a fuzzy fiber artist," I suggested.

That's where Mom drew the line. "Okay, you two, enough," she said. "This is not a laughing matter."

She was right. And I wanted some answers.

"How long have you known about this, Mom?"

"You know, I'm not going to get into this with you, Brett," she said. "Frankly, it's none of your business. Just suffice it to say Marie is my friend, and she's confided in me. And those sorts of jokes are the last thing the Pelletiers need. They need friends who sympathize, not gossip."

"I'm not gossiping; I'm just asking," I said, throwing my hands up. "Is that a crime?"

No one bothered to respond, so I decided to plunge on ahead.

"Did you know she knows Nonna?"

"Who?" they both asked at once.

"The fuzzy girlfriend," I replied patiently. "Pamela What's-Her-Face. She knows Nonna from the hospital." My parents looked surprised.

"How do you know this?" Dad asked.

"I was right there—they were talking," I said. "She said she met Nonna at the hospital the other day. She's a . . . hospice volunteer. What's that?"

"I don't remember meeting someone from hospice," Mom

said. "Then again, it was such a stressful day. . . ." Dad shrugged. His face had clouded over.

Answer my questions! I wanted to scream. A tidal wave of frustration swept over me. Then: Mr. Beady.

He was upstairs. He had just wrenched open the second-floor bedroom window and stuck his head out. We turned toward the sound, and there was his worried face looking down at us.

"Something's wrong," he said. "I can't wake her."

"Why are you trying to wake her?" Mom replied, clearly annoyed. "Let her sleep."

"No, you don't understand," he continued. "I was downstairs and heard a thump. She's fallen out of bed, and I can't wake her."

Dad was running before Mr. Beady's words fully registered with me. Mom dashed into the Gnome Home at full speed. I stood frozen, stupid, brain operating in slow motion. Move! it finally directed me, and I ran too.

I practically crashed into Mom in the kitchen. She was hanging up the phone.

"I just called 911," she said. Her face was dead pale, and she spoke deliberately. Like English wasn't my first language. "I need you to wait outside for the ambulance. Don't let them go to the wrong house." Upstairs, Dad was calling Nonna over and over, loudly.

When the paramedics wheeled her out and into the red-light-flashing ambulance, her eyes were closed. She wore an oxygen mask over her face, and they had secured her to the stretcher with wide orange straps. I suddenly felt very cold and had my arms wrapped tight around my chest.

It was like watching a train wreck, or an accident on the highway. Except this time it was happening to us.

mensch

At the beginning of every school year I bring home a pile of papers for Mom to fill out and sign. There's one we discuss together before she sends it back in: the Emergency Contact Card.

Basically, this lists the names and phone numbers of two adults they can call in case I start running a fever or vomiting during the day and they can't reach Mom or Dad to take me home. Although this might seem like a pretty straightforward thing to decide, it gets complicated.

For starters, you've got to pick someone who's home, so that eliminates all the working parents. It also eliminates Nonna, who lives at the Gnome Home only from late October to Memorial Day. Then you've got to pick someone who's a close family friend and wouldn't mind having me breathing germs or throwing up all over their house. Finally, you have to pick someone I like. And there's where the complication starts.

Emergency Adult #1 is always easy: Aunt Lorena, a.k.a. Michael's mother. A family friend who's known us since forever.

Emergency Adult #2 is always the problem. Most of my friends' moms work, or don't pass the "willing to clean up Brett's barf" test. Miss Kathy and Co. might have been a good choice, since they were right next door, but sick kids and day-care toddlers aren't a good combination.

So every year, after much argument, we reluctantly pencil in Mr. Beady as #2.

This is a serious bummer. Even on a good day—like when I score the winning goal in soccer and Mom makes tacos for dinner—Mr. Beady annoys me to distraction. He's a tease. He cracks dumb jokes. He's constantly hanging around Nonna. And he's a slob. I mean, you'd be more likely to *get* sick at his house, which is so dirty that even cats and dogs refuse to sit on the furniture.

Well. Dogs probably wouldn't mind. But cats are particular.

But as Nonna always said, and Mom and Dad agreed, "Beady is a mensch."

I remember the first time Nonna told me that. I was complaining about some stupid thing he had said to me, and she laughed.

"I don't get it," I said. "You see what a pain he is. Why is he your friend?"

"Because I've known him for years and he's the most loyal, caring person I've ever met," she said. "He's a mensch."

"A what?" I said.

"Mensch," she repeated. "*A decent, responsible person with admirable characteristics.* It's a wonderful Yiddish word that perfectly describes Beady."

"Yeah, like, I really admire the way he keeps his house," I groused.

"That's not important," Nonna said.

"Food poisoning is important!" I argued. "Fleas in the couch, sour milk in the fridge, broken glass on the floor . . . that's important!"

Nonna chuckled. "You always exaggerate for effect," she replied. "Now be honest. You know what's important. Compassion. Kindness. Generosity. And that's what Beady is all about. True, he'll never earn the Good Housekeeping Seal of Approval. And his jokes are painfully bad. But in a pinch Beady always comes through."

That conversation kept playing in my head as we sat in the hospital's waiting room the day of the Super-Sized. The Emergency Contacts had assembled: Aunt Lorena and Uncle Jack were seated in vinyl chairs near my parents, making reassuring sounds. Mr. Beady had driven over with us, behind the ambulance. He was making me insane with his pacing.

Not back and forth, but in and out. Out of the waiting room, his glance darting, birdlike, looking for the doctor who would give us news. Then, breathing heavily, impatiently, pacing back inside. A Mensch in a Pinch, I thought, and smiled in spite of everything. When Nonna woke up, I would make her laugh with this description of Mr. Beady. If I didn't strangle him first. If she woke up.

That thought had slipped unwillingly into my head while we waited. No one had said it, but there it was, this horrible idea that made my hands tremble. Made me want to throw up. Big Bad News was stubbornly knocking at the door, and I didn't want to answer.

Finally, the doctor came in.

"Okay," he said, smiling but serious. "We've had a little scare today, but we've stabilized her and she's doing fine."

He said some other things, but I only took in bits and pieces. "Keep her for observation tonight . . . dehydrated . . . talking about a garage sale? . . ." Then he told Mom and Dad that they could see her now, and they started walking out to the hallway.

"Wait!" I sounded loud after the low, hushed hospital voices we had been using. "I'm coming too."

"Hon, let us go in first," Mom said.

"No, I want to see her now," I insisted.

"Brett, wait with us," Aunt Lorena said. "Don't worry— you'll get a chance to see her."

"What's wrong? What aren't you telling me?" I demanded. I could hear the panic in my own voice.

"Mrs. McCarthy can have two visitors at a time," the doctor said briskly. He turned, and my parents followed him down the hall. I was about to dash after them, but someone held my arm. Mr. Beady.

"Wait," he whispered in my ear. "Let them get a little ahead of us." He held me like I was a puppy pulling on a leash. We watched the three of them disappear around a corner of the long corridor. Mr. Beady cleared his throat and, turning to Aunt Lorena and Uncle Jack, said, "I'm going to take Brett to the cafeteria for a cola. We'll be right back." He led me from the waiting room by the elbow.

"Now be quick and be quiet," he muttered as we power-walked in the direction my parents had taken. "We don't want them to see us . . . yet."

We tracked the doctor and my parents down several long hallways and finally to an area with a sign that read INTENSIVE CARE UNIT. Ahead was a large, open room, guarded by a nurses' station. Two women in aqua-colored uniforms stood between us and that open room. Mr. Beady frowned.

"I believe," he whispered, "that diversionary tactics are called for, Miss Brett."

I could have kissed him. Instead, I simply nodded.

Mr. Beady strode purposefully to the nurses' station counter. "Hello!" he exclaimed cheerfully. Thunderously, it seemed, in that subdued place. The women in aqua jumped, both scurrying quickly toward the loud man who didn't seem to realize there were sick people trying to sleep. A window of opportunity opened before Brett McCarthy.

I crouched low and crab-scuttled to the base of the counter. Only Mr. Beady could see me as I inched closer to the open room ahead.

"I hope you ladies can help me," he boomed. "I'm looking for a friend who was recently admitted."

"Certainly, but could you lower your voice, please, sir?" one nurse replied politely. "This is the Intensive Care Unit."

"I'm sorry . . . what did you say?!" Mr. Beady shouted. He cupped a hand to one ear. "I'm a bit deaf, *deah!*"

The sight of Mr. Beady playing the old deaf man was almost too good to miss . . . but I had a mission. Darting from the cover of the counter just as Nurse #2 joined in the attempt to shush him, I took refuge behind a row of wheelchairs in the open room.

I saw six beds arranged in a semicircle. An amazing configuration of monitors, tubes, and electronic IV setups surrounded each bed and dwarfed the patient in it. I spotted my mom, my dad, and the doctor hovering over one of them.

I unfolded from my crab position, stood upright, and tiptoed quietly toward them. The doctor was the first to see me and started to frown. That's when I realized Mr. Beady was right behind me.

"This is Mrs. McCarthy's granddaughter," he said firmly. "Give her one minute." The doctor stepped back.

Nonna looked so small. They had dressed her in a pink, flowery hospital gown, and her white hair was spread over the pillow like milkweed floss. A plastic tube was taped beneath her nose, blowing oxygen into her lungs, while an intravenous needle connected to another plastic tube was taped to the top of her right hand, feeding fluids directly into her veins. Of course, I didn't know all this at the time. To me, at that moment, it looked like aliens had gotten hold of her. Later, as time and hospital visits went on, I'd come to understand what all the gizmos were for.

Nonna was awake and smiled when she saw me.

"Brett!" she said. Her voice was raspy, like dry leaves. I could tell right off that she barely had the strength to lift her head. I wanted to hug her so badly, but all the tubes put me off. Made me afraid to touch her. I could feel tears coming, and for the first time ever I didn't know what to say to her.

She reached out to me with her untaped hand. I took it. It felt cool and soft.

"I hate for you to see me like this . . . wearing pink. With flowers," she whispered. "You know how I hate florals." Her eyes glinted up at me mischievously. "Promise me you'll run home and get my Happy Bunny nightshirt. I won't sleep a wink without it."

I saw her then. Through all the tubes and tape and pink flowers I could see my Nonna, smiling up at me, and I burst out laughing. And crying too. I bent over and gave her a hug.

"Nonna," I whispered in her ear, "you were right. Mr. Beady *is* a mensch."

pro·voked

Jeanne Anne's nose, as it turns out, was not broken. But it might as well have been. It looked like she had two black eyes. Two black-purple-and-green eyes, to be exact. The bruising across the bridge of her nose resembled a rainbow.

We both returned to school on the same day, with orders to report to Mr. Hare, the principal, before first period. They wanted us to have a little "face time" before turning us loose on the school.

Dad drove me in early. Too early for anyone to be waiting at The Junior. I hesitated before getting out of the car.

"Today won't be easy," Dad said.

"Yeah, tell me about it," I sighed. He reached over and squeezed my hand.

"But we can get through this, Brett." I pulled my hand away.

"It's important right now that we each do our part," he continued. "For you, that means getting back on track here at school. It would mean a lot to your grandmother. It's important that we don't worry her unnecessarily."

"I don't worry Nonna," I snapped. "You're the ones who worry her. You and Mom."

"Brett, please . . ."

"Why do you have to be so negative?" I said loudly. "I mean, last night . . . it was like you were planning her funeral or something. Okay, she has cancer. It's serious. But people beat cancer all the time. Nonna's tough. She'll beat this thing."

That was Mr. Beady's line. He'd said it after we'd returned from the hospital. The Super-Sized Day of the Big Bad News. When my parents finally said the C word in front of me.

Nonna had cancer. Cancer of the pancreas, to be precise. Her tan turned out to be jaundice; her brown-tail moth rash turned out to be an itchiness caused by the jaundice. Jaundice is this yellowy color that happens to your skin. It means something's not working.

No one was able to tell me exactly what a pancreas does, but one thing was clear: You can't just cut it out, like an appendix. You need your pancreas.

I heaved the door open, stumbled out of the car, and slammed it shut before Dad had a chance to reply. If I had to hear him say another word, I would explode. Little pieces, all over The Junior.

Jeanne Anne and the principal were already seated when I arrived at his office. I have to admit, I wasn't quite ready for the Rainbow Fish.

"Whoa," I said, staring.

"Yes, thank you, Brett. Please sit down," said Mr. Hare. Ironic name. The guy's bald as a Ping-Pong ball. He launched right in.

"Girls, before we can put this unfortunate incident behind us and move ahead as good citizens, we need to clear the air. Brett, I'd like you to apologize to Jeanne Anne."

I had guessed this was coming. I took a deep breath.

"I'll apologize for losing control as long as she apologizes for insulting my grandmother."

Jeanne Anne gasped.

"See?" she demanded, looking at the principal. "She's not one bit sorry!"

"Brett, are you refusing to apologize?" No-Hare asked. He sounded incredulous.

"No," I replied.

"Then . . . ?" He looked at me, eyebrows raised like little upside-down V's.

My heart raced. Go on, I thought. Make my day.

"Yes, I hit her," I said, faking calm. "But I was provoked. She owes *me* an apology."

Provoked: *aroused to a feeling or action; stirred up purposely.* She started it.

Unprecedented, yet again. In the life of Brett McCarthy, Formerly Law-Abiding Junior High Honors Student, this was a first. Flagrant disrespect for authority. Refusal to take responsibility for her actions. I didn't recognize myself.

· The little V's scrunched into a frown.

"Miss McCarthy, are we going to have to extend your suspension?" I stood up, shouldering my book bag.

"On what grounds?" I said. "*I'm* willing to apologize. She's not. Suspend her." I started walking out the door. Jeanne Anne sputtered.

"I didn't insult her! She insulted me! She . . . promoted . . . me!"

I couldn't resist that one.

"Not only are you completely unreasonable," I said, "but you're also stupid. It's 'provoked.' Not 'promoted.' " I walked out.

I had already decided that even if he called my name and demanded that I return, I'd ignore him. I wanted a scene. I wanted them to call the school resource officer and drag me— maybe even with plastic cuffs restraining my hands—down the crowded corridors. Into a waiting patrol car. Put me under hot lights. Deny me food and water until I apologized. Which I knew would never happen, because there was no way Jeanne Anne would ever apologize to *me*.

I wound through the hallway, now filled with students, toward my locker and first class. Language arts, with Diane.

She was wearing new clothes. One of those all-in-one sweater-shirt things, with the cuffs. A girl knows every item of clothing in her best friend's closet, even if she herself is mallphobic. Diane's hair was pulled back with a clip I hadn't seen before, and she wore a skirt.

A skirt. Of course. All the football players wore ties and the cheerleaders wore skirts on home game days.

I took my seat alongside her and stared straight ahead.

"Hey!" She poked my arm. "Hey, girl! Where have you been?? I've sent you, like, fifty e-mails!" I turned to her.

"Home game today?" I asked, trying to keep my voice as neutral as possible. To her credit, Diane blushed.

"Listen, we need to talk. You have no idea what's been going on. . . ."

"Oh, I think I have a pretty good idea," I said.

"No, really . . . ," she continued. "Listen, I know I should have told you about the cheerleading thing. I didn't even know if I was going to make it, you know? But there's so much more happening . . . we really need to talk."

I knew what she meant. Her world had come crashing down on her during the past week. Kit had told me.

Apparently, the evening of October 17th, the day I slugged Jeanne Anne, got suspended, and first heard the word "pancreas," the Pelletier kids got the Big Bad News. Merrill heard it up close and personal from Mr. Pelletier. They'd rented a movie and brought home dinner from McDonald's. Somewhere in between the Chicken McNuggets and the Teenage Mutant Ninja Turtles, he told Merrill that he would be living in a different house from now on, but that Merrill could visit him on the weekends. He assured Merrill that he'd like the new house: There was a dog, and another little boy almost his age. And the little boy's mother, a lady named Pamela, who was very nice.

The Pelletier women dined out that night. Mrs. Pelletier's version of the BBN was a bit different from Mr.'s. For example, she didn't use the word "nice" to describe the lady, Pamela. And she said "under no circumstances whatsoever" would Diane spend weekends at the house with the dog.

I should have heard all this myself. We should have been on the phone that night, best friends, sharing bad news the same way we shared Gifford's Moose Tracks ice cream. Separate spoons, but both digging out of the same container.

Instead, I turned the computer off that night . . . and every night of my suspension, cutting off Diane's only means of communicating with me since The Ban on phone calls. I knew her life had just unraveled, that her whole world had been redefined. But I was too wrapped up in my own BBN to be anybody's BFF.

Before I could reply to Diane, the Rainbow Fish entered. There were little gasps across the room as people got a look at her face. She stopped at my seat.

"Mr. Hare told me to give you this," she said. She held a sheet of white paper aloft, then dropped it, letting it flutter slowly to my desk. It was typed on front-office stationery. It said I had lunch detention at the principal's office every day, indefinitely.

I folded the letter neatly in half, then ripped it along the crease. Then I ripped the two halves into quarters. Into eighths. Sixteenths. Jeanne Anne stared, her mouth dropping open.

The class was dead silent, watching us, and the sound of tearing paper seemed unusually loud.

"You are *so* getting into trouble for that!" Jeanne Anne exclaimed.

"Getting into trouble for what?" Language arts teacher approached.

"Brett ripped up a detention letter from the principal!" she declared. Language arts teacher frowned.

"Jeanne Anne, take a seat, please. Brett, is that true?"

Redefined Brett McCarthy put on her best clueless face.

"I don't know what she's talking about," I said innocently. Jeanne Anne, bless her, took the bait.

"Liar!" she shrieked. "You know I just handed you a letter and you ripped it up!" Language arts teacher picked up a few scraps.

"I can't read this," he said impatiently. "Brett, what is it?"

"Old homework," I said, looking straight into his eyes.

"You lying *witch*!" Jeanne Anne yelled. That did it. Especially because the teacher thought she'd said something way worse.

"Jeanne Anne!" Language arts teacher was pretty mad. "We do not use that sort of language in this classroom! Pack up your things, young lady. Follow me. The rest of you . . . sustained silent reading until I get back!"

"What'd I do? She's lying!" Jeanne Anne was pretty close to tears. "Call the principal. Call him right now. He'll tell you. . . ."

The old me might have felt a little sorry for Jeanne Anne at that point. Bruised, multicolored face. Totally losing it. Hauled off by the teacher while the real criminal played innocent.

But this was Brett McCarthy, Redefined, and I didn't have a whole lot of sympathy in reserve. I ducked my head to hide the smile as Jeanne Anne and the teacher left the room, as I heard her finally burst out crying once they reached the hallway. I searched my backpack for a sustaining book. Diane stared at me. Shocked.

"What's going on with you?" she asked. As if I knew.

"Shh!" I said, putting my finger to my lips. "This is supposed to be *silent* reading." I buried my nose in my book and didn't look up until language arts teacher returned.

A long time would pass before Diane and I spoke to each other again.

pen·sive

Here's the thing about detention letters: You can rip them up, but you can't ignore them forever. Eventually they catch up with you. Kind of like former best friends.

It turns out my fight with Jeanne Anne set off an earthquake in the eighth grade. Shifted the tectonic plates of our little world, so now there was this big rift, the Mescataqua Grand Canyon, with some kids on one bank and some on the other.

In other words, people took sides.

This was really obvious at lunch. Mom didn't have time to pack my lunch today, so I was buying. As I came off the food line with my tray of chicken fries and chocolate milks, I realized I had nowhere to sit. Our table—the Kit, Diane, Brett, and (unfortunately) Jeanne Anne table—was now occupied by a group of Band Jocks. I hesitated, looking over the sea of heads for an empty chair next to someone who still liked me. Someone from the same circle of Hell.

"Brett!" Kit was waving at me from the back of the room, the long table usually filled by girls from our soccer team. Gratefully, I steered myself toward her at a near run.

That's when I realized just how much had changed. As I wove through the maze of tables, almost every kid I passed greeted me; and not always in the—shall we say—most *pleasant* way. There were high fives, some *Welcome back, Brett!*s and even some guy who shouted out, "McCarthy rocks!" But there were hisses and catcalls too. I heard *Loser!* more than once, and from one table—I'm convinced it was Darcy's crowd of starving somersaulters—someone pelted me with a doughy bread ball, which landed on my tray.

I slid next to Kit, who promptly picked up the bread ball and hurled it, hard and with amazing accuracy, in Darcy's direction. Kit plays baseball on the *boys'* junior high team, so no one tossed it back.

"That was different," I said. "Thanks for saving me a seat."

"No problem," she said. "D'you see where Diane is?"

Instinctively, I turned toward Darcy's crowd. Sure enough, at a small table near them I picked out the back of Diane's new sweater, the sun glinting off her perfect licorice hair. She was near the windows, eating lunch with a guy. The guy. Bob Adonis Levesque. And their heads were bent close together in what seemed to be a very friendly conversation.

"Whoa," I said, unprepared for the second time that day. "When did that happen?"

"During your suspension," Kit replied. "What, she didn't tell you? I figured you were going to fill *me* in." I shrugged.

"Oh, c'mon!" Kit prodded me with her elbow. "Give it up. Whaddya know?"

"I'm banned, remember? Her mother won't let her call me."

Kit stared. "You're serious, aren't you? You haven't talked to Diane. All this stuff has come down, and you've let a *phone ban* get in your way? What gives?"

First Michael, now Kit. Why was everyone so amazed that I didn't have up-to-the-minute info about Diane Pelletier's life? Did it ever occur to them that I might have other things to think about?

"Do *not* tell me this is about cheerleading," Kit said.

"You think it's cool that she's gone over to the Dark Side?" I demanded. "You are the most anti-cheerleader person I know! You call them Bulimic Butt Wigglers!"

Kit looked pensive.

Pensive: *musingly or dreamily thoughtful*. Thinking about what I just said.

"You know," she finally sighed, "you're right. I think cheerleading is stupid and I have called Darcy a Bulimic Butt Wiggler. Frankly, she is. But this is *Diane*. She's awesome."

"People change," I said. Where had I just heard that? Oh, right. Michael.

"C'mon, Brett," said Kit. "If it makes her happy, why should we care? Besides, it was only a matter of time. She's

117

gorgeous, and she can do handsprings without messing up her hair."

Before I could reply, the loudspeaker cut through the noise of the cafeteria.

"Would Bettina McCarthy please report to Mr. Hare's office? Bettina McCarthy."

Of course. My detention. I was supposed to be dining with the principal.

There's a reason why human beings invented nicknames. It's to make sure that people whose birth certificates say something like . . . like Hilda or Percival or Bettina can make it through life without being emotionally scarred. For most of my life, "Brett" had saved me from the humiliation of "Bettina." Now, thanks to the women who worked in the front office, my cover was blown.

At first no one had any clue who Bettina McCarthy was. But a few geniuses figured it out when they saw me pick up my tray and head for the exit. They started banging on the tables, chanting, "Tina! Tina!" and within seconds the whole room took up the beat. It was a little scary, actually. How I imagine a riot would look in a maximum-security prison. I could see teachers and lunchroom aides glancing around nervously.

I made for the shortest route to the exit doors, which, unfortunately, led me right past the future homecoming princesses (Darcy's posse), the romantic darlings of Mescataqua Junior High (Bob and Diane), and a long Guy Table filled with the Smoking Demigods of Cool (Bob's friends).

I fixed my eyes on the exit but couldn't help hearing the hisses and insults from Darcy's crew. Couldn't help noticing that Bob and Diane were among the few people in the cafeteria *not* pounding or yelling, just silently watching me go. Couldn't help overhearing one Demigod, whose clueless comment just about said it all:

"Bettina?" I heard him ask. "I thought her name was Josephine."

mon·u·men·tal

The free fall my redefined life had taken might have stopped at that point *if* I had headed straight to No-Hare's office. But instead of trotting off to the principal, I made for the lockers, grabbed my backpack, and left the building. This, as it turns out, was a monumentally stupid choice.

Monumental: *massive; outstanding; very great.* Incredibly huge.

Taking off from school without permission is practically a federal crime. We're talking Office of Homeland Security, Bomb-Sniffing Dogs, and Search and Rescue Helicopters. When a junior high kid disappears, adults go into panic over-drive. Apparently they combed the building, interrogated kids, called my parents, and finally put out an all-points bulletin with the police for a missing eighth-grade girl.

I was, of course, at the Gnome Home, unaware of the havoc I had caused. Watching soaps and eating the leftover chocolate-raspberry-chip brownies Nonna and I had baked a few days earlier.

Just as the closing music and credits rolled, signaling the end to that afternoon's episode of *The Young and the Restless*, Dad arrived. He pushed the kitchen door open with such force that it banged against the wall and made me jump. If that hadn't been enough to give me a heart attack, the look on his face sure was. A foreboding combination of rage and panic.

"Would you mind telling me what you're doing here?" he demanded.

"Eating cookies and watching TV," I replied instantly. True, but smartmouth, nonetheless.

"Home. Now!" he boomed. My dad never booms. "You have some serious explaining to do!"

The Spanish Inquisitor, looking somewhat less furious and a whole lot more scared, waited in the kitchen.

"Are you aware," she said in a choked voice, "that half the Mescataqua police force is out looking for you?"

"I'll call the school and tell them we found her," said Dad. He disappeared into his study and closed the door. I closed my eyes, took a deep breath, and braced myself for the Lecture of a Lifetime. When I turned to face my mother, I got just the opposite.

Her face crumpled. She put her hands over her eyes, and tears slid between her fingers. She sobbed without making a sound. Until you've made your own mother cry, you just don't know misery.

In Michael's and Dante's defining circles of Hell, I had officially slipped from the Seventh Circle, the Violent, to the Ninth Circle: Traitors to Family. I would pencil it into his Fifth Period notebook myself.

Dad spent a long time on the phone in his study before rejoining us in the kitchen. He wasn't booming anymore and he seemed a whole lot scarier.

He had the following Big Bad News: I was suspended again (a full week this time). I was grounded (not that I had anywhere to go). Most importantly, Mr. Hare had decided to bar me from playing soccer for the last few weeks of the season. Not even practices.

"Wait a minute! Can he do that?" I said, feelings of extreme guilt pushed aside by panic. "I mean, he can keep me from games while I'm suspended, but the rest of the season?"

"He just did," Dad said quietly.

"No way!" I exclaimed. "Kids do worse things than cut school and they still play. He's wrong."

Dad cleared his throat. "Mr. Hare has my full support on this decision," he said. "I think this might be a good way to get your attention."

"Dad . . . please. You have my attention, okay? I'm sorry. I shouldn't have left school. Mom"—I turned to her—"I'm so sorry. I know . . . this is the last thing you need right now. We're *all* upset. But please, don't make things worse for me. I need this."

Dad frowned. "You need soccer?"

How could he possibly understand? He never played sports in school, never played on a team. He'd been one of those Gifted and Talented sorts himself. Mom had been an art geek. They had no clue what it felt like to stand at the corner of an emerald-green field, wind up, and boot a ball in a perfect crossing arc. Hear the roars and cheers from the crowd. I searched for language my college-English-professor dad could understand.

"It's not just a game, Dad. It . . . *defines* me."

His face resembled a mask. His spoke quietly, without a trace of emotion.

"Well, that's a problem, isn't it?" he said.

ig·no·min·i·ous

Mr. Beady took me that evening to see Nonna. It was her last night in the hospital, and she was anxious to go home. Well, more like *demanding* to go home. Once they'd got some fluids into her, and finished running all their tests, she claimed she felt like her old self.

"Beady, you've gotta get me out of here," she chirped the moment we entered her room. She was sitting straight up in bed, on top of the covers. She wore her cozy magenta chenille socks and one of the Happy Bunny nightshirts we'd brought from home. Her half-eaten dinner was pushed aside ("These people cook worse than *me*!" she'd declared) and her night table was crowded with big vases of flowers and about a zillion crayon colorings from the Kathy kids.

"We'll spring you *tomorrah, deah*," he chuckled, settling into the vinyl armchair beside the bed. "Cheer up. Miss Brett and I brought you an Italian from Emilio's."

I sat on the edge of her bed and handed her a paper bag

containing a twelve-inch submarine sandwich stuffed with ham, pastrami, salami, provolone, shredded lettuce, onions, and peppers. Nonna grinned, reaching inside. "Oil and vinegar, salt and pepper," I said.

"I adore you," she said. "Your mother brought bran muffins today. They're in the drawer. Take them on your way out."

Mr. Beady and I watched silently as Nonna tucked into her Italian. Her McCarthy appetite had returned, although her jaundice remained. It would take some time, the doctors told us, for her color to improve.

"Did you bring the forms we talked about?" she asked Mr. Beady between bites.

"Yes," he said hesitantly. "But wouldn't you rather visit with Brett instead of filling out forms?"

"I don't mind," I said quickly. The last thing I wanted to do was talk about my ignominious day. A Mr. Beady word I'd looked up.

Ignominious: *characterized by disgrace or shame; dishonorable*.

"Go on, Beady," said Nonna. "I'd like to see what she thinks, anyway."

Mr. Beady sighed and pulled a sheaf of papers from an inside coat pocket. He placed it on the bed alongside Nonna.

" 'Taking Charge of Your Health Care,' " she read aloud. " 'Maine Health Care Advance Directive.' "

"Translate?" I said. Nonna wiped her fingers, flipped a page, and read on.

" 'When you need medical care, you have the right to

make choices about that care. But there may come a time when you are so sick that you can't make your choices known. You can stay in charge by putting your choices in writing ahead of this time. This is called giving advance directives.' "

"Oh," I said. Maybe talking about my ignominious day might be preferable. Even though I had direct orders from my parents *not* to tell Nonna about the second suspension. An unprecedented move, since I always told Nonna everything. But our redefined lives had new rules, apparently, and Not Upsetting Nonna had become Rule #1.

"Maybe you should wait until Mom and Dad are around to do this," I suggested.

"She tried," said Mr. Beady. "They fought."

"Since when do you fight with Mom and Dad?" I said. So much for Rule #1.

"Well, it wasn't exactly a *fight*," Nonna explained. "More like a tearful disagreement. For one thing, I want to be an organ donor. That wasn't a big problem for them. You all know how I'm into recycling. But I also want a Do Not Resuscitate order, and that upset them."

"That means if her heart stops beating, or she stops breathing, she doesn't want the doctors to do CPR and all the rest of it," Mr. Beady translated.

"Why not?" I asked, trying to keep my voice as neutral as possible. It was hard not to show how much this conversation was freaking me out.

"Because when the ol' ticker stops tocking," Nonna said,

patting her chest, "I'll assume it's time to go. And I want that to be peaceful."

" 'Do not go gentle into that good night,' " Mr. Beady said in a gravelly voice.

Nonna frowned. "Not yet, Beady. No Dylan Thomas yet," she said. Mr. Beady rose from his chair and wandered to the side table packed with vases.

" 'Wasteful, weak, propitiatory flowers,' " he sighed, fingering the petals of a large daisy. I saw him glance slyly at Nonna, waiting for her reaction. She didn't disappoint.

Nonna snatched up the empty sub bag, rolled it into a ball, and threw it at him.

"That's it! Out, Beady," she exclaimed. "Go get yourself a cup of coffee from the machine. I warned you: No Philip Larkin, especially *that* poem. Give me some time alone with my granddaughter."

Mr. Beady, beaming and not looking one bit repentant, gave me a little wave and left the room. Just as Michael was to movie lines, Mr. Beady was to poetry. Add a poetry-quoting dad to the mix, and it was enough to drive a person insane.

"Now, where were we?" Nonna smiled as the door closed.

"Who's Philip Larking?" I asked, hoping to change the subject.

"Larkin. Philip Larkin," she said. "A British poet, and I can't stand him. Beady loves his work. The only thing he might enjoy more than reading Larkin is torturing me about Larkin. It's an ongoing battle."

"Are there other families on the planet that fight over poems?" I wondered aloud.

"I certainly hope so!" she said. "What else is worth fighting over, except perhaps love and politics?"

I sighed, stretching myself across the foot of her bed. "You want to know what I can't stand?" I said. "I can't stand the way Dad says 'poem.' Most people just say it like 'pome.' Simple. But Dad says it 'po-ehm.' Like it's got two syllables. Drives me nuts."

Nonna looked thoughtful. "I think it does have two syllables," she replied.

"No way," I said.

"Yes way," she persisted. "I really think it does. It's subtle, but it's definitely a two-syllable word. *Po-ehm.* Look it up when you get home."

"Oh, god, are we really talking about poems and pronunciations?" I moaned, hands over my eyes. "You people are weird and making me weird too. I'm doomed."

"Well, you brought it up," Nonna said brightly. "Since you don't seem to want to talk about my advance directive."

I didn't reply.

"What is it about discussing these forms that bothers you?" Nonna asked.

"Nonna . . . duh!" I exclaimed. She looked startled.

"I beg your pardon?" she said.

"I don't want to talk about you dying!" I said. "I think that should be a no-brainer, okay?" I rolled onto my stomach and hung my head over the edge of the bed. The blood rushed to my ears. Nonna and I stayed like that for a while.

"Brett, look at me," she finally said. I rolled over.

"I owe you an apology," she said carefully. "In so many ways you seem so wise and mature to me that I talk to you as if you're an adult. That's not fair, and I'm sorry."

"It's okay," I said.

"I don't want to talk about dying either," she declared. "I want to talk about living. I have a lot of living left to do, and I'll need your help in getting it all done. But Brett . . . living is not the absence of dying. Dying is part of the deal. We all do it—some better than others, if you want my opinion. And I want to die the way I've lived." We let that sit for a while before either of us spoke again.

"I don't know what you mean," I finally said.

"Give it some thought," she said. "In the meantime, I have a proposal for you."

Then Mr. Beady, with his knack for interruptions, returned.

"What'd I miss?" he asked, resettling into his vinyl resting place.

"We're planning a party," Nonna told him.

My eyes widened in surprise. Nonna never spoke sarcastically to Mr. Beady, no matter how annoying he was. But then I realized: She wasn't being sarcastic.

dire

The actual substance of junior high is so mind-numbingly dull that people yearn for little scandals to think about. Even a falling-out between once-obscure, Pluto-circling BFFs was enough to set e-mails flying.

So when I finally returned to school after my second suspension, Diane and I provided plenty of material for the rumor mill simply by ignoring each other. Anytime we took up space in the same room, eyes focused on us, everyone waiting for a fight or a snarly comment.

But week after week: nothing. We passed in the hallways, handed test papers to each other in language arts, changed for gym at adjacent lockers: nothing. Our worlds had come crashing down—Kit told me Diane's parents were having fights in public places, like the grocery store parking lot; she told Diane my Nonna had cancer—and we said nothing. "You're *both* being idiots!" she complained, but I simply shrugged.

What Kit didn't get was that Diane and I now existed on different planets. Coupledom with Bob, plus cheerleading, had launched her into stratospheric levels of popularity. You could practically hear the cameras clicking when she walked down the halls, the eager paparazzi of Mescataqua Junior High watching—and imitating—her every move. If her home life was in shambles, if she was crying herself to sleep every night, you'd never have guessed it. She seemed more beautiful, more perfectly positioned smack-dab in the middle of The Junior, than ever before.

Meanwhile, her former BFF, former Best Eighth-Grade Corner Kicker in Maine, was . . . bored silly. Climbing the walls every gorgeous, crisp fall day after school as my soccer team practiced without me and boarded the yellow bus on game days and headed off together in a chanting, riotous pack. Okay, so it was probably unreasonable of me to expect them to wear black armbands and go into mourning because Brett McCarthy got kicked off the team. But my girls didn't seem to miss a beat. They even won games without me. The nerve.

To make matters worse, I had a date with the principal every day. A lunch date, that is. While Diane munched lettuce leaves at the Impossibly-Thin-Way-Popular-Girls' table, I got treated to a daily gag fest with No-Hare. Lunch detention required that every day I drag my sorry self and my sandwich to his office, where he would sit behind his desk, eat cafeteria fried chicken, and lick his fingers.

Luckily, he didn't talk much. I had feared a mini Lecture of a Lifetime each day, but No-Hare seemed perfectly comfortable with our companionable silence, broken only by his swallowing, chewing sounds. Usually he read while he ate. I'd wolf down my PB&J, then knock out some homework until the bell rang.

One day we had company. Walking into his office at lunchtime, I discovered Mrs. Augmentino, the school's Gifted and Talented coordinator.

"Ah, here she is! Come in, Brett," No-Hare said jovially, in his Company Voice, that hearty, fake voice adults always use when "company" is around. Something's up, I thought, settling into my usual chair and unwrapping my sandwich.

"How are you, Brett?" asked Mrs. Augmentino, sounding very sincere.

I shrugged. "Okay, I guess," I said. "How are you?"

"Well, actually, I'm very excited," she replied. "Someone special paid me a visit this morning. Can you guess who it was?"

Oh gosh golly! I wanted to exclaim. Can you say, "Special Visit," boys and girls?

Mrs. Augmentino has this really annoying habit of talking like a female version of Mr. Rogers. It sends Michael into major Mr.-Rogers-imitation mode after every Fifth Period.

"Uh, I have no idea," I replied instead.

"Really?" she persisted. She seemed truly surprised that I didn't know.

"Really," I said, taking a big bite of my sandwich.

"Your grandmother, of course." She smiled. I almost choked.

"And her friend," Mrs. Augmentino continued, unaware of the dire effect of her words. "An elderly gentleman named Mr. Beady."

Dire: *desperately urgent; warning of disaster.*

"Why?" I sputtered, mouth full.

"Your grandmother has come to us with a marvelous Special Challenges project proposal," Mrs. Augmentino explained. Special Challenges, a.k.a. Fifth Period. That's what the teachers call it. I enjoy telling Michael he's challenged.

I imagine I looked pretty challenged as Mrs. Augmentino filled me in. I think my mouth dropped open and my bag lunch fell unnoticed to the floor when I learned that Nonna and Mr. Beady had come up with the idea to set the Nerd Herd loose on the lighthouse problem. Their question: How would you illuminate a lighthouse without electricity, solar panels, lead acid batteries, a Fresnel lens . . . in other words, how did they do it back in Thomas Jefferson's day, when Spruce Island light was built?

This was exactly the sort of stuff that got the Fifth Period's mental machinery humming. It was Odyssey of the Mind, Destination Imagination, and Math Counts all rolled into one. With Michael and company on the case, I reckoned we'd see that lighthouse ablaze come summer. Take that, Maine Maritime Academy.

"Brett, you haven't answered Mrs. Augmentino's question," No-Hare said, dragging me back into the conversation.

"I'm sorry . . . what?" I stammered.

"I said, how would you like to participate in this project?" she repeated.

"I'm not in Fifth Period," I replied automatically. I am Brett McCarthy, I thought. Former Soccer Star, Violent, Practically Friendless *Nongenius*.

"Yes," replied Mrs. Augmentino, reading my thoughts. "But we thought since this involves your family, you might like to join us. And you know, Brett, you're quite a capable student. One of your former L.A. teachers—Mrs. LaVoie—has spoken very highly of you. I think you'd enjoy a Special Challenge."

"I've already consulted the guidance counselor, who says we can easily accommodate this schedule change for you," No-Hare said. "You'd have to switch lunchtimes. Eat with the Special Challenges class . . . I know, you'll miss me. You'll also lose your study hall."

No more giggling Diane and Jeanne Anne passing notes in study hall? No more dining with No-Hare?

"Where do I sign up?" I almost shouted.

"Excellent!" No-Hare looked satisfied.

"Marvelous!" Mrs. Augmentino enthused. I realized it had been a long time since one of my decisions had pleased an adult, let alone two.

The bell rang, signaling my release, and as I hurried through the halls to my next class, I could feel the grin stretched across my face. Because there was no way, no *way*, he'd know I'd been invited to join their group. I laughed to myself as I sprinted toward my locker, imagining Michael's expression when Brett McCarthy, Special Challenges Scholar, strolled into Fifth Period.

prow·ess

I wasn't the only one who'd had no clue what Nonna and Mr. Beady were up to. My parents shared my cluelessness. But I didn't fully appreciate *how* clueless until dinner that night.

Even though my new membership in the Fifth Period club had nothing to do with my mind (Mrs. Augmentino had carefully chosen "capable," not "gifted," to describe my intellectual prowess) and everything to do with Nonna's involvement, I couldn't wait to tell Mom and Dad.

Prowess: *extraordinary ability.*

Deep down, I think my folks always wondered where they'd gone wrong. Maybe if they'd made me take Suzuki violin lessons, or played classical music while I did puzzles, or spoken Spanish to me in the womb, I would have turned out to have an IQ like Michael's. Or like theirs. Instead, they got a poorly dressed sports nut, and while I knew they loved me, I also knew they didn't quite *get* me.

So I figured they'd be thrilled to see me in Fifth Period.

Hangin' with the smart kids. Maybe some of it would rub off . . . could genius be contagious? . . . and instead of IM'ing Kit or watching back episodes of *Lost* on TV, I'd spend evenings discussing *po-ehms* (two syllables) with Dad.

But here's the thing about parents: Just when you think you've got them figured out, they pull the rug out from under you.

They greeted my big news with: silence. The spinach lasagna steaming on our plates made more noise.

"Well, let's get excited, why don't we?" I finally said.

"I—I'm sorry," Dad stammered. "Mother never said a word to me about this."

"And that surprises you?" Mom replied sarcastically.

"It's actually not a bad idea," Dad said. "That's a pretty creative bunch of kids. And with our Brett"—he reached over and squeezed my shoulder—"I bet they'll come up with a great plan." He smiled, but I saw worry behind his eyes.

"Did the teacher mention whether Nonna plans to attend these classes?" Mom asked.

"She didn't say. And I haven't asked Nonna." The Gnome Home had been dark when I'd gotten home from school that afternoon.

"Well, great. Just great," Mom snapped. Tossing her napkin into her full plate, she got up from the table and walked over to the sink.

"What'd I do *now*?" I exclaimed. Somehow, my marvelous news had soured.

"You haven't done anything, sweetheart," Dad said. "We're just a little frustrated with your grandmother right now."

"Because?" I prompted.

"It's complicated," Dad said. "She has some decisions to make about her treatment, and we're having a hard time getting her to focus." I remembered the forms Nonna had had with her in the hospital. She'd seemed pretty focused to me.

"Mr. Beady said you guys fought," I said.

"Mr. Beady needs to mind his own business!" Mom burst out. Dad flashed her one of his "not-in-front-of-Brett" looks. Typical.

"Beady seems to be her partner in crime these days," Dad said dryly. "I know he has her best interests in mind, but for a man in his seventies he can be rather immature. About certain things."

"Such as?" I asked, a tad aggressively. For some reason, it bothered me to hear them criticize Mr. Beady.

"Such as this *ridiculous* party he's cooked up for her!" Mom fumed. "Did he tell you about this . . . this Bazooka Birthday?"

I had heard. We'd started planning it during Nonna's last night in the hospital. Instead of talking about the advance directive forms (which would upset me) or my latest suspension (which would upset Nonna), we'd planned her birthday party. Nonna would turn seventy-three in December, and she had some very definite ideas about how we should all celebrate.

For starters, no gifts. "The last thing I need is more *stuff*," she declared. "I need to get rid of stuff, not take more on."

"Don't we all," Mr. Beady commented. Nonna's face brightened.

"Beady, you're brilliant!" she exclaimed. "That's exactly what we'll do!"

"I said something brilliant?" he asked me. I shrugged.

"Instead of a gift, everyone has to bring something they need to lose," Nonna said.

"But then won't you get stuck with all *their* stuff?" I asked. Probably pretty bad stuff too. I had some fairly awful socks I needed to toss.

"No . . . we'll blast them! From the bazooka!" Nonna said excitedly.

"What if they bring old cars? Bicycles?" Mr. Beady asked.

"They'll have to bring small items," she said. "Or photos of larger items. Or models. Symbols." Nonna was on a roll. She began to think out loud. "Perhaps the things they want to lose are not material at all—what if someone wants to lose weight? Or a bad habit? The possibilities are endless!"

The whole wacky idea pleased her enormously. For the rest of that evening we talked party: from the menu to the guest list to all the stuff we imagined people bringing. We planned until the night nurse told us visiting hours were over, and as Mr. Beady and I drove home, I realized we hadn't thought about cancer for an entire hour.

"You know, the party is not Mr. Beady's idea," I told my parents. "This is all Nonna. And she's psyched."

"The party is fine," Dad said tiredly, as if this were a topic he'd already discussed a million times. "But we can't let it distract us from what's important right now."

"Exactly," Mom agreed. "And that means treatment. Meetings with doctors. Visits to the hospital. I know those things are not as much fun as planning parties or . . . building lighthouses with children . . . but being a grown-up means doing a lot of boring things. It means taking responsibility."

"You sound like you don't think Mr. Beady and Nonna are grown-ups," I said quietly.

"That's right. Sometimes I feel like I've got *three* children!" Mom exclaimed. Dad slapped his fork down loudly on the table.

"Enough," he said firmly. "I will talk to Mother. Tonight. I'll find out what she's planning at the school and make sure it coordinates with the treatment plan the doctors have prescribed."

"Fine," Mom said, clearing away our half-eaten plates. "As long as she starts chemo next week. That's priority number one."

i·ron·ic

Growth is a defining fact of a junior high kid's life. *The* defining fact.

Early growers are Royalty. Kings and Queens of the school dances. Lords and Ladies of the sports teams. Once-skinny boys who could barely heft a basketball from the free-throw line morph into broad-shouldered starters for the A team. Shy girls who only just gave up playing with dolls sprout bodacious breasts requiring hot outfits from the teen department.

Conversely, slow growers are Peasants. In a world where everyone wants to seem as high school as possible, flat-chested shortness is a curse. Lucky slow growers find a safe haven in Geek World, too busy practicing their musical instruments or attending math meets to worry about the boy-girl or sports scenes. The unlucky . . . those who are short, untalented, and only mildly intelligent . . . they kind of get lost in junior high.

It was ironic that just when everything in and around me

concerned growth, my grandmother embarked on a journey of *anti*growth, a.k.a. chemotherapy.

Ironic: *given to irony; expressing something other than and especially the opposite of*.

The doctors wanted to shrink the tumors they'd found on Nonna's pancreas. So they prescribed chemotherapy. Chemo, as Mom called it. This involved Nonna going to the hospital once a week, where they fed antigrowth chemicals into her veins. The chemicals stopped the cancer cells from growing—as well as all the other cells in her body. Her fingernails. Her hair. *Bam!* No more growth. And the thing about hair is that when it stops growing, it loses its hold in your skin. And it drops off. Not all at once, but slowly. First a few extra hairs in the brush or on the shower floor. Then handfuls. And before you even realized what had happened, your silver-haired Nonna was bald.

Unfortunately, chemo also causes nausea. Which causes vomiting. Which causes weight loss. So another irony of that winter was that while I spent most of my waking hours feeding my machine with healthy foods (*not* Pop-Tarts), and waking up every morning a bit bigger, Nonna shrank. Pounds fell off her, she slept a lot, and because she didn't feel well, she didn't speak as much. Even her personality seemed smaller.

She had cut a deal with my parents: She'd do chemo for six weeks and see how it went. She wouldn't skip her treatments and she'd follow all the doctors' orders. In exchange, they'd leave her alone about participating in the lighthouse project.

My first day in Fifth Period coincided with Nonna's first

chemo treatment, so she didn't come to school. Mrs. Augmentino said I could "intro" the project for everyone. She asked me to bring pictures of the island and come prepared to speak.

Nonna was really happy that I'd been invited to join the lighthouse project, and not just because it gave me something to talk about besides missing soccer. The night before my presentation we pulled together about a dozen of our favorite Spruce Island photos and glued them to poster board. I practiced what I'd say about each, and in what order. We figured a visual prop like that would keep me from panicking, which was a real possibility.

That's because despite my unbelievable confidence and aggression on a playing field, I am an absolute wreck when publicly speaking.

"Don't look at the audience," Nonna advised me. "Pick a spot on the back wall and talk to it like it's an old friend. Works like a charm." She'd offered this advice after we'd finished the board and started in on the Congo Bars she'd baked. I passionately adore Congo Bars.

"What's the occasion?" I asked, selecting a particularly large bar from the plate.

"Chemo Eve," she replied matter-of-factly. "My personal Mardi Gras, if you will. The big pig-out before you can't eat." She helped herself to the next-biggest bar. I didn't need to ask what she meant. We'd already had a family talk about her treatments.

Nonna and I sat silently chewing. Chemo Eve had turned frosty—the weatherman had predicted our first dip into the twenties that night—and she'd fired up the woodstove. The dry logs popped comfortably as we ate and surveyed our photo display.

"That one's my favorite," I said, pointing to a four-by-six of me, Mom, Dad, and Nonna. Each of us held live, unbanded lobsters in each hand as we posed for the camera. I must have been about five, but I was fearless when it came to lobsters. The sun shone brilliantly in that picture, and all the colors—ocean blue, balsam green, windbreaker yellow—were vivid.

Nonna nodded. "That was a happy day," she agreed. "This one's my fave." She pointed to a fading Polaroid of her, Dad as a little boy, and my grandfather standing outside one of the cottages. Weeds grew high around the front steps, and the clapboards dropped paint in curling gray peels. The place looked a mess.

"Why that one?" I asked.

"It takes me back to a good time," she said simply. "We were broke, with more work on our hands than we could handle. But we had each other and our health. With all our years and all our dreams stretching before us."

"Yeah, but you didn't have *me* yet," I teased.

Nonna placed one hand on my shoulder and squeezed. "Oh, yes we did," she said. "You were the dream."

Arriving at the Fifth Period door, poster board tucked under one arm, I tried to keep my mind focused on the business at hand and not on what I imagined happening that very moment in the hospital across town. Nonna's parting words to me on Chemo Eve kept running through my head.

"We will both be very brave tomorrow," she'd promised, hugging me good night at the kitchen door. Not "try to be brave," but "will be brave." Cowardice not allowed.

I scanned the room for Michael. He still had no idea that I was joining the ranks of the Gifted and Talented. I couldn't wait to see his expression. It was the only thing, other than Nonna's expectations of bravery, preventing me from turning tail and running away from all those bright young minds.

Michael's back was turned when I walked in, and there was a vacant seat behind him. I slid quietly into it, leaned forward, and whispered, "Yo, Einstein."

Michael whirled around, his jaw dropped, and I could almost hear the well-oiled gears in his finely tuned brain screech to a halt. *This does not compute! This does not compute!* screamed his inner hard drive.

"Guess who's Specially Challenged?" I said. Before he could answer, Mrs. Augmentino strode into the room.

"Good morning, boys and girls!" she trilled with enthusiasm. "I am *very* excited today. Not only because we begin a new project, but also because we welcome a new classmate. Brett McCarthy, could you come to the front of the room?"

Delight instantly turned to dread as fifteen pairs of eyes fixed on me and my poster. My feet felt like they'd been tied to lead weights as I shuffled forward. *Be brave,* I thought. *Be brave.*

"We're beginning a unit on islands this month," Mrs. Augmentino said. "Maine's coast includes thirty-five hundred islands—did you know that?—and in addition to looking at the unique history, biological diversity, and extraordinary microclimates of our island communities, we've come up with an expeditionary project for those of you who would like to take the challenge!"

Mrs. Augmentino could have been speaking Greek. This is bad, I thought. Where were the Smoking Demigods of Dumb when you needed them? My heart raced in panic as Mrs. Augmentino went on. I looked at Michael, but he was listening intently, nodding his head with interested comprehension.

"Brett?" Mrs. Augmentino gazed at me expectantly. Fifteen pairs of eyes shifted back to me. Oh help, I thought.

"I'm sorry . . . what?" I stammered.

"I said why don't you tell us about your family's island," she said kindly.

I unrolled the poster Nonna and I had made and clipped it to the easel Mrs. Augmentino had set up. Stare at the back wall, a little voice said in my head. But no way could I force myself to face that room full of geniuses. I turned instead to the photos, desperately trying to remember the opening lines I'd rehearsed.

It was as if someone had tossed me a rope. The smiling faces of my family and the bright colors of Spruce Island pulled me in, and suddenly I wasn't thinking about how stupid and out of place I felt. I wasn't thinking about the hospital or Nonna's treatments. I was smelling salt water. Listening to foghorns and seagulls. Picking wild blueberries.

"For me, Spruce Island is the most amazing place in the world," I began. "But it's not for everyone. There's no electricity, so we don't watch TV. There's no running water, toilets, or showers, so we carry buckets from a hand pump, pee in a privy, and wash from a basin. We have propane for cooking and refrigeration, and we heat with woodstoves. But the cottages aren't insulated, so you can't stay there in winter. There's no trash service, so we compost our food scraps and burn what we can. There's no bridge, so we come and go by boat. When you're out there, you feel completely cut off from the rest of the world. You feel different."

After that I didn't notice how nervous I was. I told them every story that went with every picture on that poster. About the grandfather I never knew. About the fairy houses Mom and I would build in the woods, using moss, pinecones, and twigs. About cooking lobsters and clams over an open fire on the beach, covering them with seaweed to keep the steam in. I forgot about the time or the room full of kids.

"For my family," I said, finally out of breath, "Spruce Island isn't just a place where we go. It's a way to *be*. When we return to the mainland, we use TV and electricity again. But we keep a little bit of Spruce Island inside us, and it feels good to know that we'll always go back." The bell rang.

"Whew!" Mrs. Augmentino exclaimed. "That was more

than any of us expected. But it was wonderful, don't you all agree?" Fifteen pairs of hands burst into applause. Michael put two fingers into his mouth and whistled.

"For tomorrow I'd like each of you to come up with one unique fact about Maine island life. And, for those of you who decide to take the Lighthouse Challenge . . ." Mrs. Augmentino's voice rose to operatic heights of excitement. "Think up one way to light a lighthouse. Actual or imagined. As Brett told us, the Spruce Island light hasn't been used in many, many years. And for our expeditionary project some of you may design and actually construct a functioning light."

The final bell rang and everyone began shuffling out. I was rolling my poster when a girl approached me.

"Have you ever been to Monhegan Island?" she asked earnestly.

"Uh, no, actually," I said. "But I've heard it's cool."

"You made me think of it when you described the fairy houses you make with your mom," she continued. "People build fairy houses all over Monhegan. Fairy villages, practically. They're really wonderful. You should check them out sometime." She stood looking at me, waiting for a response.

"Yeah, I'll do that," I said. I waited for her to go away.

"Your presentation was very good," she continued. "Your family is very lucky."

"I know," I said. "I mean, about being lucky. Thanks."

She stuck out her hand.

"I'm Monique Rose," she said. "Welcome to Fifth Period." We shook hands, and Monique Rose departed.

Okay, I thought. I guess I made a friend. Then someone behind me cleared his throat.

"So . . . how'd I do?" I said as we left the room.

Michael's smile stretched wide across his face. "Can you say 'challenged,' boys and girls?" he replied in his Fred Rogers voice. "Can you say 'awesome'?"

im·pas·sive

The stamping on the bleachers sounded like thunder. The rhythmic roar of "De-FENSE! De-FENSE!" shook the walls of the gym. It rattled the cartons of Milky Ways, Skittles, and Three Musketeers neatly arranged on the shelves of the Snack Shack. Or, to be more accurate, the Snack Closet, an impossibly small space in the junior high lobby where you can buy candy, soda, popcorn, and pizza during basketball games. The girls' basketball team runs the Shack during boys' games, and the boys run it when the girls play.

As a member of the Mescataqua girls' basketball team, I had volunteered, with Kit, for this, the boys' season opener. We were both sorry. It had turned out to be an amazing game—the Mescataqua Maineiacs versus the Topsfield Buccaneers, our archrivals—and with three minutes to go in the fourth quarter, the score was tied. Both of us were dying to abandon our Snack Shack posts and join the screaming crowd in the gym, but we knew we'd get in big trouble if we turned our backs on all the food, not to mention the cash box.

So we had decided to take turns, one of us standing at the gym entrance, reporting the scores sportscaster-style to the one stuck in the Shack. With two minutes to go, Kit was stationed at the entrance and I struggled to hear her above the noise.

"Okay, our ball!" she yelled. "Ty Davis is driving hard down the middle . . . they're pressing! They're pressing him hard! Pass! Look, look . . . he's open!" she yelled.

"Who's open?" I shouted. Kit kept forgetting I couldn't see a thing.

"Excuse me. Can I have a popcorn?" A little boy, no bigger than Merrill, stood at the counter holding a dollar bill.

"Yes! Yes!" Kit screamed. The mob in the gym roared.

"What? What?!" I yelled.

"A popcorn!" the kid repeated, loudly. Kit was jumping around like the floor was a hot griddle. I grabbed a large-size popcorn carton, scooped it full, and thrust it at the little kid.

"I want a small one," he said.

"Take a big one," I snapped impatiently. "Go on, you can have it for free. What happened?!" I shouted at Kit.

"You're weird," said the kid as he walked away.

"Time out," Kit called. "Oh, man, this is so close. . . ."

"Kit, if you don't tell me what happened, I'm gonna lose it!"

She trotted over to the Shack. "The Bucs are pressing. Hard. They were all over Ty Davis, he came to a complete stop near the middle of the court, I swear, he was going to lose it, when Bob Levesque broke free from his man, Ty *rolled* it to him, Bob flew down for the layup, hit it, and got fouled! Three-point play!"

"He made the free throw?"

"Oh . . . not yet. The Bucs have called a time-out. But he will!" She bolted back to the entrance as the horn sounded. There is no way I'm missing this, I thought. Grabbing the Snack Shack keys off the hook, I slammed the door, locked it, and ran over to Kit.

"C'mon," I said, grabbing her arm and pulling her into the gym.

Before my redefinition as a two-timer in the suspension club, I would never have abandoned my post selling junk food in the Snack Shack. True, the old me was no goody-goody; I made my share of mistakes. But I had always *tried* to follow the rules.

But those days were over. In early December of my eighth-grade year "the rules" no longer made any sense. Nice guys didn't necessarily finish first. Mean, rotten people got to be popular. Being good didn't mean good things would happen to you. Because if it did, then nice people like Michael and Monique Rose and the others in Fifth Period wouldn't get teased. And my Nonna, the best human being on the planet, wouldn't have ended up bald and skinny and vomiting from cancer drugs. Unable to eat her Thanksgiving dinner, or even get out of bed.

Kit and I managed to squeeze into the bottom-row bleachers just as Bob squared up for his free throw. Some Buccaneers on the other side were barking like dogs and waving their arms, trying to distract him. Bob calmly bounced the ball three times, eyes on the hoop, knees bent, compressed for the shot. He let it fly. . . .

Nothing but net. Our fans erupted.

I saw the furious shake of green-and-white pom-poms way at the other end of the bleachers as the cheerleaders bounced like, well, cheerleaders. I wondered if any of them actually knew the rules of basketball. As the screaming from the fans died down a bit, I could hear them chanting.

"Bob Levesque! He's our man! If he can't do it, no one can! Goooooooo Bob!"

While they shrieked their special Bob cheer, Diane stepped from the line. She had put aside her pom-poms and was running, full tilt, arms extended over her head. Then, without anyone to spot her or a soft, cushy mat beneath her, she began handspringing before the entire length of bleachers. Over and over, at breakneck speed, finally ending in a complete flip, a perfect stop, a perfect satisfied smile. The Smoking Demigods of Cool, at least the ones who weren't playing, roared appreciatively from the stands.

She was utterly, flawlessly beautiful and amazing. I had no idea how she did it. I could sink free throws and three-pointers all day, or direct a soccer ball into a goal with laser accuracy. But complete a forward roll, let alone a tumbling run at sixty-five miles per hour? No way.

"You go, girl!" screamed Kit, jumping up and pumping her fist in the air. I could feel myself wanting to applaud as well. But I stifled the urge and focused on the game instead.

Bob's three-point play had ignited the rest of the team; they couldn't do anything wrong after that. They started running down the clock, breaking free of the Bucs' press and just passing, passing, passing the ball, forcing the Bucs to foul them and then swishing their free throws. When the buzzer finally sounded, it was Mescataqua Maineiacs 54, Topsfield Buccaneers 45. The gym shook.

"Let's get back!" I yelled in Kit's ear, pointing toward the lobby. We sprinted out the double doors and made it back to our posts just as the first wave of departing fans lined up for candy and soda.

After ten minutes of selling pandemonium the crowd cleared out and Kit and I started shutting down the Shack. Unsold popcorn tossed, pizza warmer unplugged, that sort of thing. We were almost done when a few members of the team, flanked by girls still wearing their cheering uniforms, approached. Bob. Ty Davis. Diane and Jeanne Anne. I was suddenly really busy stacking candy cartons on the back shelves.

"Awesome game, you guys!" Kit exclaimed, high-fiving Bob and Ty.

"Are you closed?" Bob asked.

"Only to the general public," Kit said. "Star athletes and gymnasts may still purchase candy and drinks." Everyone laughed.

The guys bought Cokes. Jeanne Anne bought some chocolate and chattered aimlessly with Ty, who didn't seem to be paying attention to a thing she said. She was doing a great job of pretending I wasn't there. We had both perfected the art of ignoring each other's existence, which suited me fine. Diane stood at the entrance, indecisive. I pushed a carton of Skittles toward her on the counter. Her favorite.

"Oh, great," she said. "I'll take two."

"That's probably her dinner," joked Bob. "Better make it three."

"Shut up," she said, smiling as she fished around for change in her backpack. The guys popped their Cokes and drifted toward the exit doors as Diane counted out quarters and dimes. I took a deep breath. Like I was about to duck my head under water.

"That was really cool," I said. "That handspring thing you did."

"Yeah, save it, Brett," she replied shortly.

"Huh?"

"I don't need a hard time from you, okay? So save it," she said quietly.

I could feel my face burn. "I wasn't giving you a hard time."

Diane flashed me a yeah-right glance as she stuffed the Skittles into her backpack. "Whatever," she said, walking away.

At that instant the outer doors opened, and in walked Mrs. Pelletier. Her eyes darted, looking for Diane.

"Hey, hon. Ready to go?" She was wearing a black skirt and nice shoes, like she had just come from work. She had tired circles under her eyes. Diane nodded, calling out her goodbyes to everyone as she headed for the doors. Then Mrs. Pelletier saw me.

"Brett!" She came striding over. "How are you? How's your grandmother?"

She used The Voice. Not a whisper, but quiet. Friendly, but not cheerful. Sympathetic. Interested. The way adults spoke whenever they asked about Nonna.

"She's okay. Thanks for asking." I had learned to say that. Thanking them helped cut the conversation short. Assuring them that Nonna was fine seemed to make them feel better. Less guilty. Not that there was anything they could do. But they all acted sort of guilty, like they should have been bringing over meals and get-well cards but hadn't gotten to it yet.

"That's great," Mrs. Pelletier replied, relief in her voice. "I keep meaning to get over there, but . . . well, you know how it is." I didn't, actually, but I still nodded. I just wanted her to shut up and go away.

"Do you need a ride home?" she offered.

"No," I replied instantly. "Dad's picking me up. But thanks."

The idle chatter in the lobby had come to a complete halt. Everyone had stopped pretending to look out the windows or tie their sneakers or adjust their backpacks. They just listened.

"Well, tell your mom hi from me and let her know if she needs *anything* . . . just call."

Mrs. Pelletier headed out the doors, and Diane followed, shouldering her pack. Just before they disappeared into the black night, Diane turned. Our eyes locked, and I had this impression of water between us. Like we were floating in the same big ocean but in two separate lifeboats. Neither of us spoke, and her eyes were expressionless. Impassive.

Impassive: *giving no sign of feeling or emotion.*

It made me wonder what she saw in my eyes.

ex·as·per·at·ed

"Well, what did you expect? Did you think one nice compliment would make up for two months of ignoring each other?"

It was a few days before the Bazooka Birthday party, and Michael had come over to humiliate me at Ping-Pong. I let him do this every once in a while; it's the only sport he beats me at. As we batted tiny white balls back and forth over the net, I told him about my run-in with Diane at the basketball game.

"Of course not," I replied. "But I didn't expect her to just march off, either." I popped the ball up high to his forehand. Not smart.

Michael crooked his arm behind his head and spiked the ball swiftly into my backhand. He plays Ping-Pong like he was born and raised in Beijing, China.

I ducked under the couch to retrieve the ball. It was cracked. The third one that morning.

"Be nice," I said, holding up the disabled ball. Michael pulled another from his pocket and we started over. *Tap-pock*.

Tap-pock. Occasionally *blahtt!* whenever I set it up high for one of his slams. I hate the sound of Ping-Pong balls.

"I guess my question is what's your goal?" Michael said as we hit.

"How do you mean?" I asked.

"I mean do you *want* to be friends with Diane again?"

"Sure," I said instantly.

"Really?" Michael said. He caught the ball. The playroom seemed oddly quiet without the annoying *tap-pock*. "You want to eat lunch with Jeanne Anne and Darcy, maybe add a few of Bob's friends to your Buddy List, and spend Saturdays at Abercrombie and Fitch?"

"Who?" I asked, totally confused.

"Aahh!" he exclaimed, and pretended to bang his head on the Ping-Pong table. "Not who. What. They're a store. *It's* a store."

"And your point is?" I asked irritably.

"My point is that while those girls practically live at the mall, you can't tell the difference between Abercrombie and Fitch and . . . and . . . Rosencrantz and Guildenstern! While they're shopping, you're practicing free throws. While they're painting their toenails, you're building Ped-o-Sleds in your grandmother's garage. Don't you get it?"

"I don't get what this has to do with Diane," I said. I tossed my paddle on the table and flopped into the overstuffed couch. Michael sat next to me. He wore his "let-me-explain-this-to-you-stupid" expression.

159

"You're not like them. Diane is."

"Not true."

"She is."

"She's not."

Michael let out an exasperated sigh.

Exasperated: *irritated, annoyed.*

"You've got to let go of this, Brett."

"What, you mean give up? Give up on a friend?"

"Give up on pretending you have to save her," Michael said. "I hate to break this to you, but she seems perfectly happy in Jeanne Anne World. Accept it. Move on."

Jeanne Anne World. It was as if Michael had said, "Lights! Camera! Action!" and I could see vivid images of thin girls with their hair pulled back tight, wearing stylish clothes from . . . Rosenstern and Guildencrantz. Girls with nail polish and smoking boyfriends. Girls who could do cartwheels on balance beams. Who had as much in common with me as the man on the moon.

"So you think there's no chance Diane and I will ever be friends again?"

"Probably not," Michael said. "Not the way you used to be, at any rate." There was silence between us.

"I hate this, you know?" I finally said, tears in my voice. "The way everything is changing?" I didn't need to define "everything" for him.

"Yeah," he agreed. Then Michael did something that totally shocked me. He shifted closer on the couch, so that our legs touched, and wrapped his arms around my shoulders. He rested his chin on top of my head, and I realized with a surprised little jolt that he was bigger than me. Somehow, when I wasn't looking, short, skinny Michael had hit a growth spurt. Go figure.

But here's the even more shocking thing: I didn't push him away. I felt myself lean back into the couch, into him, and relax. I felt all this tension flow away, my muscles unwind, and I closed my eyes.

"You are so cool," he said quietly into my hair. "So many people like you."

"Yeah?" I said. "Like who?"

Michael lifted his head and looked into my eyes. "Kit. Your soccer, basketball, and lacrosse teams. Practically the whole Fifth Period. Really, Brett, everyone keeps asking me if you'll stay on after the lighthouse project is done."

I felt a little surge of pride. He was right. True, I wasn't a math whiz, or a science genius, like some of them . . . but I wasn't a dope, either. Apparently they thought I was a really good storyteller, and on the days when we had to "share" our notebooks, they'd applaud after I read my entry.

"Where'd you learn to write like that?" Monique Rose had asked me. I remember the day. Fifth Period had just ended, and we were walking together to gym. It had been my turn to bring the Surreptitious Snack: my term for Food You're Not Supposed to Eat in the Hall. This had gotten to be our thing, Monique Rose and I, sneaking snacks on the way to gym.

"Write like how?" I'd asked, tearing open a foil pack of Fruit Roll-Ups and looking over my shoulder to make sure there wasn't a hall monitor in sight. I unwound one long snake of rubbery goo, ripped it in half, and handed her a piece. She chewed thoughtfully.

"With your senses," she finally said. "When you describe things, I don't just see them. I can hear them. Smell them. Taste them. I mean, next time I eat a lobster, I'll be thinking, 'So, is this both sweet *and* salty, like Brett says?' "

I shrugged. It was hard for me to imagine how someone like Monique Rose, who'd already taken the SAT twice and scored high enough to get into college, thought my scribbles were anything special.

"I don't know," I said. "It's just what I do. But I'll tell you what. When you come to the island with us next summer, we'll eat lobsters and then you can decide whether I know what I'm talking about." Monique stopped walking. She even stopped chewing.

"Are you inviting me to the island?" she asked quietly.

"Of course you're invited to the island," I replied. "There's an acre of woods that's perfect for the Fairy Condo Complexes I know you're dying to build." She hesitated for a moment before giving a little squeal and throwing her arms around my shoulders.

"Oh my god. This is *so* cool!" she said when she finally released her hold on me. "You have no idea how much I wished you would ask me. I mean, it sounds so incredible, and so beautiful. . . ." Monique Rose enthused all the way to gym.

Michael was right and I should have left it at that. Should have accepted his compliment, wiped my eyes, and picked up the Ping-Pong paddle.

Unfortunately, I have a big mouth. A big sarcastic mouth with a mind of its own. And sitting on the couch like this with him was more than I could handle.

"Great. So now I'm Queen of the Geeks. Next thing you know, I'll try out for Destination Imagination," I quipped.

I felt him stiffen, then pull away.

"You need to stop that," he said flatly. There were two red patches on his cheeks.

"Stop what?"

"Einsteins, Brainiacs, Nerd Herd Honchos, the Great Gifted Wonders . . . it's not funny. We have to listen to that stuff all day in school, and I don't expect someone who is supposedly my friend to pile on. Especially when we've let you in."

"Excuse me? We? I thought Mrs. Augmentino let me in."

"I don't mean literally. I mean . . . as a friend."

"Geez, no need to get so sensitive!" I replied. "You know I don't mean anything by it, and hey . . . Monique Rose and I even have sleepover plans this weekend. I mean, I'm an official member of the Geek Lovers of America now." I burst out laughing at my own joke.

"I'm outta here," Michael said, getting up from the couch.

"Oh, c'mon, lighten up!" But he was finished. Without another word Michael climbed the basement stairs. I heard the kitchen door open and close, signaling his departure from the house.

"Fine, be a jerk," I said.

It struck me that I was talking to myself.

dis·si·pate

"Michael's mad at me."

I spilled this to Nonna one afternoon while we made cappuccino brownies spread with cream cheese frosting and topped with a dark espresso glaze. Enough caffeine in a single brownie to give you the zooms for days.

It was Thursday, the best day of her week. Fridays were treatment days, a.k.a. anti-growth-chemical days that left her weak and vomiting. Usually right on through the weekend, by Monday the sickness slowly dissipating until she felt almost normal on Thursday. Then back to the hospital again for another round.

Dissipate: *to fade; slowly drift away.*

"I don't think I've ever seen Michael mad at anyone," said Nonna. "Are you sure?"

"Yup."

Nonna wiped her hands on a dish towel. She went over to the cupboard and took out two small plates and glasses. From

165

the pan of newly frosted, high-test brownies she carved two hunks and put them on the plates. She poured milk into the glasses and pointed to the kitchen table. We sat.

"Speak," she said.

"He got pissed off," I sighed. "I called the Fifth Period kids geeks. I didn't mean anything by it. He just took it the wrong way."

"It is rather unkind," Nonna said. "And undeserved. I find the Fifth Period group to be very friendly." Nonna had joined Fifth Period on Wednesdays, her next-to-best day of the week. She didn't really do much, just moved from group to group remarking in amazement at what the class had accomplished.

Rather than strange and full of themselves—which they had every right to be—most of them were pretty nice. They dove into their projects with gusto, indifferent to whether their enthusiasm made them look cool or not. Out in the regular pool of classes a lot of them were usually quiet. During Fifth Period they were unleashed.

"I know. I like them too," I told her. "I didn't mean anything by it. I call Michael 'Einstein' all the time, and he knows I'm not saying it to be mean."

"Does he?" Nonna asked. "Sounds to me like his feelings were hurt. You of all people know that words are powerful things. We have to choose them carefully, especially with friends."

We chewed in silence for a while.

"Nonna, do you think I'm a lousy friend?" I finally asked.

A big knot had formed in my throat, and it wasn't brownie. Nonna put her hand over mine.

"I think most junior high girls are lousy friends." She smiled. "Actually, I'd call you a friend-in-training. You're just learning how to be a friend, and you're making lots and lots of mistakes along the way."

"I used to be a good friend!" The tears came for real now. "First Diane. Now Michael hates me. Kit's probably next. I'm hosed."

"What happened with Diane?" Nonna asked gently. "I wondered why she never comes around anymore."

"It's complicated." I sniffed, wiping my nose on a scratchy paper napkin. "She's really into this cheerleading thing, and a whole other group of girls. And she has this *boyfriend* now. I don't really fit into her new scene, you know?"

"I'd imagine her new scene isn't all a bed of roses," Nonna commented. "I hear her parents' divorce has gotten quite ugly."

"I know," I sighed. "Kit says she's wrecked. But I was so mad that she blew me off that . . . I never even asked her. We've never spoken about it."

"Well." Nonna let out her own sigh and leaned back in her chair. "You've had some upheaval in your life too, don't forget. All of this . . ." She rubbed her nearly hairless scalp. "None of you complain, but I know it's not easy."

"Everything has changed, and I hate it!" I burst out, tears returning. "I hate hate hate it! I want it to stop!"

Nonna burst out laughing.

"Don't we all! But change happens. Redefinition happens. Darling, we are works in progress. Every one of us."

"Well . . . it sucks!" I shouted.

I'm not supposed to say "sucks." My parents get on my case big-time about it and Nonna says it makes me sound crass. At the moment, however, it felt like the perfect word to describe my life.

I waited for the inevitable reprimand. Then Nonna surprised me.

"Yes, it sucks," she replied calmly. "Sometimes. Other times it's wonderful. We can't always control it. But we *can* control how we react to it. I mean, look at me. Did I think I'd celebrate my seventy-third birthday looking like Tweety Bird? Some mornings I wake up and wonder, 'Who made me a member of the Cancer Club? I'm not one of those sick people!'" Nonna shook her head and laughed in quiet amusement. "It's like when your grandfather died. I remember sitting in church at his funeral, wearing a black dress I had borrowed because I never owned anything black, thinking, 'There's been a mistake. I'm not a widow. I'm not all alone with this little boy.'"

"But you were," I whispered. "Were you scared?"

"Terrified. Furious. Just so mad at life you wouldn't have recognized me. But Brett, somewhere along the way you have to stop being mad and get back to business. Think of what I would have missed if I'd crawled into a hole after your grandfather died! And cancer? That's something that's going on in my body, but it's not who I *am*. It doesn't define me."

Nonna took a big bite of brownie. She closed her eyes and chewed slowly, savoring it.

"Ask yourself: Are things going to happen to me? Or am I going to head out and make things happen? If you want to be a good friend, then go out and *be* a good friend. Don't let anything stop you. Not cancer, divorce, or even cheerleaders." She took a swig of milk.

"Amazing," she said. "You know, I can't cook. But I work miracles with chocolate."

per·cep·ti·ble

Although you start learning about drugs and alcohol in elementary school, teachers don't kick it into high gear until junior high. No more coloring books from Mothers Against Drunk Driving, or visits from McGruff the Crime Dog. In junior high they pull out the heavy artillery: namely, Officer Hotchkiss.

Once a week we had Officer Hotchkiss for DARE class. As in Drug Awareness Resistance Education. We would file into the Health and Family Sciences room, where Hotchkiss would wait, dressed in full law-enforcement regalia, even down to the gun holstered at his hip. He had a Marine-issue crew cut, three rolls of skin on the back of his neck, and a little dirt-line mustache. The guy never smiled.

He never cracked a joke. He never sat down. Ramrod-straight and stern, he'd spend forty minutes describing all the horrible things that would happen to us if we got caught dealing drugs, using drugs, or driving drunk. He didn't take questions; he didn't ask questions. He didn't want answers because *he had* all the answers. He was one scary guy.

Here's the other thing about him: He didn't like the smart kids. You'd have thought he would, since the smart kids generally *weren't* potheads. But early in the year—with that not-so-smart-guy's radar for high IQs—Hotchkiss had identified Michael and a couple of his Fifth Period cronies. He'd go out of his way to reprimand them, or embarrass them, for the least little thing. It made you wonder: Had gangs of Gifted and Talented students beaten him up on the playground when he was little?

The day before the Bazooka Birthday, Officer Hotchkiss was detailing the various penalties for marijuana use and possession in Maine. It was all I could do to keep my eyes open. The previous week had been highly entertaining—he had brought in slides featuring mug shots of his favorite criminals and told us all about how they'd ruined their lives through drug use. This, however, was a big snooze.

He had just droned out the penalties for growing marijuana plants at home (six months in jail and a $1,000 fine for five plants or less; ten years in jail and a $20,000 fine for more than five hundred plants) when Michael raised his hand.

"Excuse me, Officer Hotchkiss, but you haven't mentioned medical marijuana."

"Come again, son?" Hotchkiss asked.

"Twelve states have laws that permit medical marijuana. Maine is one of them."

Hotchkiss didn't answer right away. An unfriendly smile formed beneath the dirt line.

"Well, I'm sorry to disagree with you, young man, but we don't have any special laws for doctors who smoke pot." Laughter rippled across the room. I saw red creep across Michael's face. But he didn't back down.

"No, of course not," he said firmly. "But in 1999 Maine decriminalized marijuana use for people who have their doctor's permission. In Maine a sick person can have up to one and a quarter ounces of marijuana, and grow up to six plants."

"Cool," said a voice from the back of the room, eliciting more laughter.

"That'll be enough!" Hotchkiss said sharply. He turned to Michael. "In *very* rare cases Maine turns a blind eye to marijuana use by *some* patients. But the vast majority of users are engaging in a very dangerous, illegal activity, and *will be prosecuted* under the law."

A hand went up. "Why would sick people use marijuana?" Michael dove right in.

"There's a chemical in marijuana known as THC," Michael explained. "It helps reduce pain and nausea and even increases your appetite. It really helps people with cancer who have been doing chemotherapy treatments and losing weight."

"So, like, it gives you the munchies?" came the back-of-the-room voice again. Wild laughter.

"Well, yeah. That's right," Michael replied.

"Enough!" barked Hotchkiss. "There is absolutely no evidence that smoking marijuana helps. In fact, it hurts. It's much worse than cigarette smoking and can give you cancer." Obviously, Hotchkiss *did* know more about this than he had let on.

"Well, that doesn't make any sense, does it?" Michael said matter-of-factly. "I mean, if you're already dying from cancer, why not smoke a little pot if it helps? Like I said, it's perfectly legal in Maine and eleven other—"

"I said enough!" Hotchkiss repeated loudly. You could have heard a mouse sneeze, it was that quiet. Michael looked surprised.

No clue. He had no clue how much like a little professor he sounded. He might be getting laughs, and good questions, as a result of his informed comments. But nobody loved him for it. Basically, junior high kids hate know-it-alls. Even well-intentioned know-it-alls. And I suspected that emotionally, Officer Hotchkiss had not advanced much beyond his own junior high years.

"This is not a joke!" Hotchkiss said severely, glaring at Michael. "Pack up your things. I'll speak to you in Mr. Hare's office after class."

For one stunned moment Michael just stared at him. Then he slowly began to stuff pencil, notebook, and loose papers into his binder. He kept his eyes fixed on the floor. I think it was the first time in his life that Michael had ever gotten into trouble at school.

Brett McCarthy, no stranger to trouble, stood up.

"Excuse me," I said clearly. "Why are you sending him to the office?"

"Have a seat, please," Hotchkiss said icily. "This does not concern you."

"Yes, it does," I said. You could have heard a pin drop in that room. This was turning out to be more entertaining than the inmate slides.

"And how is that?" Hotchkiss asked sarcastically.

"My grandmother has cancer. She's lost a lot of weight because she's nauseous from her treatments. If smoking pot could help her, I'd like to know."

"The medical benefits of marijuana are questionable, and the harm caused by marijuana is very well known!" Hotchkiss insisted. "Now, unless you'd like to join your friend here in a trip to the principal's office, I'd suggest you have a seat."

Hotchkiss had no clue that dates with the principal were nothing new to me. I didn't budge.

At the back of the room a new hand shot up. Bob Levesque.

"I think Brett makes a good point. After all, it's legal. Right, Mike?"

A chorus of "Right, Mike?"s filled the room. I remained standing. Michael had stopped his shuffle toward the door and looked across at me. I tried to smile at him without really smiling. Like tossing him an imaginary rope.

Another hand up. Monique Rose.

"If *smoking* the pot is a problem, what about *eating* it? I was watching a movie recently about the sixties, and people were baking marijuana into brownies. Might that work, without the side effects from smoking?"

An enthusiastic round of "Right!" erupted from every corner.

History Dude, a Fifth Period kid who was to history as Michael was to math, answered her without even bothering to raise his hand.

"You'd have to determine whether the heat from the oven destroys the THC," he said.

"Right," she said.

"Yeah! Right!" someone exclaimed.

"Actually, there's a way to extract THC from the marijuana leaves," Michael said excitedly. He'd obviously forgotten that he wasn't floating in his safe Fifth Period pond right now but swimming with the piranhas. "It's not as potent as smoking it, but there are some benefits. And doctors can prescribe it in capsule form."

"You mean pot pills?" someone asked. "Right, Mike!"

Hotchkiss looked furious. He opened his mouth to say something dire. Instead, the bell rang.

"You!" Officer Hotchkiss said loudly, pointing at Michael while the whole class rose and began the swarm to lunch. "You're still headed to the office!"

I felt my knees unlock. At the back of the room Bob was laughing and high-fiving his Demigods, "Mike" already forgotten. Diane, in the seat next to his, rose slowly. She glanced my way, and I wasn't sure, but it seemed like she nodded. A barely perceptible tip of the head. Then she walked out.

Perceptible: *capable of being noticed.*

In the hallway I scanned the crush of faces. You could lose sight of someone within seconds when the lunchtime crowd was on the move. Then, only a few locker lengths away, I found what I was looking for. I pushed through the sea of shoulders and book bags and grabbed hold of Michael's elbow.

"Hey," I said. "Going my way?"

in·so·lence

That night Michael and I found ourselves searching Web sites for pro and con arguments in the medical marijuana debate. This was Principal No-Hare's solution to the DARE class disruption issue.

Unlike Officer Hotchkiss, No-Hare had the greatest respect for high-achieving students like Michael. He'd also gotten pretty chummy with me. Once soccer season ended and winter set in, he surprised me by showing up at a few of the eighth-grade girls' basketball games, then catching up with me in the school hallway the next day to talk hoops. Turned out that he was a huge North Carolina fan. True, his lip-smacking, finger-licking ways with fried chicken could turn the strongest stomach. But anyone who loves the Tar Heels couldn't be all that bad. So when Hotchkiss complained about Michael's drug-promoting insolence, No-Hare was skeptical.

Insolence: *insultingly contemptuous speech or conduct; impudence.*

To make Hotchkiss happy, No-Hare promised to "punish" Michael with an assignment: Come up with ten pro and ten con arguments in the medical marijuana debate. And since I just happened to be standing around and Hotchkiss told him *I* had been involved too, he included me in the assignment.

Michael was thrilled. He loved research. He suggested we go online at seven o'clock and IM each other as we gathered the twenty arguments.

We were almost done when I got a shocker: A message from Diane popped up.

2Di4: hey.

I stared at it, stupidly, for at least thirty seconds. She knew I was online. I had assumed she'd deleted me from her Buddy List months ago. Obviously she hadn't, which meant every time she'd been on the computer, sending messages to all her cheerleader pals, she'd have been able to see whether Sockr-gurl was on. Likewise, I'd never deleted her. Just watched, as night after night she entered and exited cyberspace. It was like spying, with binoculars, from the windows of a tall building as Diane came and left from another building across the street. And we'd both been doing it.

Sockrgurl: hey back.

2Di4: whazzup?

Sockrgurl: not much. u?

Then Michael sent a message.

MensaMan: BINGO!!

Sockrgurl to MensaMan: what's bingo?

MensaMan to Sockrgurl: just found #10 con. we r done!

Sockrgurl to MensaMan: awesome. we r done.

2Di4: thought u & m were brave 2day. hkiss is a loser.

MensaMan to Sockrgurl: want 2 play checkers?

Michael is big into online games. He's especially into chess, sometimes playing three or four games simultaneously with grand masters across the globe. He usually invites me to play something more commonplace, like checkers or crazy eights.

Sockrgurl to MensaMan: u always win. no fun 4 me.

Sockrgurl to 2Di4: thx. it was mostly m.

Carrying on two separate Instant Messenger conversations is not easy, especially when one conversation is from a long-lost-friend-turned-enemy and the other is with a recently-hurt-reconstituted-friend. My head began to ache.

MensaMan to Sockrgurl: i'll let u win.

2Di4 to Sockrgurl: howz your nonna?

Sockrgurl to MensaMan: still no fun.

Sockrgurl to 2Di4: not great.

MensaMan to Sockrgurl: i'll let u win and play 4 money.

2Di4 to Sockrgurl: sorry 2 hear that.

Sockrgurl to 2Di4: u r 2 wierd. i'm blocking u.

Sockrgurl to MensaMan: thx 4 asking.

There was a long pause; nothing from either of them for a full minute. Then:

MensaMan to Sockrgurl: u r welcome. does that mean yes or no?

It took me several seconds to realize I'd sent each of them the other's message. But there it was, right on the screen.

Diane wrote back.

2Di4 to Sockrgurl: b that way. i was trying 2b nice.

"No!" I yelled, pounding the countertop with my fist.

"Someone having trouble with her homework?" Dad remarked calmly from behind his newspaper.

Sockrgurl to 2Di4: don't go please!!! I'm on w/m 2. that message was 4 him!!

She didn't see it. The little lower right-hand corner message box floated up, announcing that 2Di4 had just signed off.

MensaMan to Sockrgurl: checkers?

"Aah!" I yelled in frustration. This was too stupidly ironic. I reached for the phone and dialed the Pelletiers' number.

"Hello?"

I recognized her voice. "Diane, don't hang up. This is Brett. Let me explain."

"You've got thirty seconds," she said calmly.

"Okay, just now? I was online with Michael. We had to do a project tonight about marijuana—No-Hare assigned it 'cause Hotchkiss was really mad—and we were messaging back and forth, and then you came on just as we finished and Michael wanted to play checkers. See? And I was trying to tell him no at the same time as talk to you and he was being a pain. So I told him I was blocking him, but by accident I sent that message to you. I absolutely didn't mean to call you weird. I meant Michael."

Long pause.

"Okay, that was so confusing and ridiculous that it *must* be true," she finally said.

"It is. Believe me," I said.

"Okay," she said. Another long pause.

"Thanks for asking," I finally said. "About Nonna."

"Yeah, well I wondered how she's doing. We just got an invitation to her birthday party."

Second surprise of the night. I had no idea Nonna had invited the Pelletiers.

"Really. Are you coming?" I asked.

"Would you like me to?" Diane asked.

"Sure, if you'd like to. But I have to warn you: It's gonna be bizarre."

"I'm used to bizarre. My whole life is bizarre," she said. I think she sighed.

"Well . . . great. About coming, I mean. Not about your life," I said.

"I've got to go," she said suddenly. "I'll probably see you at the party. Tell Michael for me that I thought he was brave. Bye, Brett." She hung up.

Meanwhile, Michael had sent about twenty messages. He could tell I was on and couldn't understand why I didn't reply. I grinned as I scrolled through them all.

"What the heck," I muttered, typing.

Sockrgurl to MensaMan: i feel invincible tonight. wanna play chess?

ag·i·tat·ed

Until Diane told me *she'd* been invited, I had no idea how far the Bazooka Birthday invitation list extended. Neither did my parents. They had grudgingly agreed to the party and had even been helpful and not-grouchy about the whole thing. Until they got a sense of the size. Super-sized.

"Did you know Nonna invited the Pelletiers?" I asked them the evening Diane and I spoke. Right after Michael had finished trouncing me in three successive games of chess. Mom frowned.

"I had no idea," she said. "She doesn't really know Marie that well, does she?"

"Makes you wonder whom else she invited," Dad mused. He and Mom exchanged the Significant Look. I knew nothing of interest would be said in my presence once Significant Looks began, so I excused myself and went to bed. I figured we'd know soon enough how many people were descending on the Gnome Home.

As I poured about a pint of syrup over two Eggo waffles the next morning, watching lazy white flakes float to the ground outside the kitchen window, Mom slammed through the door. Her cheeks bright red from the cold, she stamped snow from her boots, yanked off her coat, and tossed it on a chair.

"We have a problem," she declared. "She's even invited the nurses from oncology. There's no way all those people will fit in that little house. And we're due for a foot of snow." She strode into Dad's office, where I heard muffled, agitated words exchanged behind the closed door.

Agitated: *excited and troubled in mind or feeling.* Stressed.

Nonna's guest list totaled 123 and included the Kathies, Fifth Period *plus* Mrs. Augmentino, five oncology nurses, all the neighbors, Nonna's book group, hiking club, and Elders United for Peace and Social Justice group, Mr. Beady's bird-watchers, Dad's entire department plus their spouses and kids, Mom's quilting group, the Emergency Contacts, and every random friend within a fifty-mile radius. Even I could appreciate what a logistical nightmare this posed.

The solution: bonfires. Once Mom and Dad finished panicking, they got on the phone and called everyone they knew who owned backyard bonfire dishes. Before lunchtime, six had been delivered to our door, and Dad arranged them along Nonna's driveway and throughout her yard. Meanwhile, Mom went to Wal-Mart and purchased a few miles of outdoor Christmas lights, which she set me to stringing between the

Gnome Home garage, the house, and the trees. Inside the garage she arranged Coleman stoves on a few long tables, with huge pots that would contain hot chocolate, warm cider, and mulled wine. If guests couldn't fit *in* the house, then the party would have to spill *out* of the house.

Nonna was thrilled.

"It'll be like winter carnival," she enthused, watching from her window as Mom and Dad worked frantically to get everything into place. I had taken a break from light stringing to help her arrange sweets on platters.

"Nonna, where did you think all these people were going to sit?" I asked her.

"I honestly never thought about it," she replied. "But you see . . . everything works out, doesn't it?"

As Mom and Dad worked outside, I shoveled the last of the brownies onto a serving tray. Nonna had opted for brownies instead of cake. When it came time to sing "Happy Birthday," she wanted everyone to have his or her own treat with a candle, so each of us could blow it out and make a personal wish. Those were the sorts of details she'd planned ahead; not how to accommodate one-hundred-plus guests.

By late afternoon Team Bazooka arrived, a.k.a. Mr. Beady and Michael. They positioned the bazooka, along with a table where they could stack blastable items, just outside the Gnome Home living room windows. Nonna would watch from there, in a comfy seat next to the fireplace. The weeks of chemo had robbed her of "insulating blubber," as she called it, and now she was always cold. No number of bonfires would keep her warm enough to view the blasting from outside.

I went outside to inspect Team Bazooka's progress. One little wrapped gift was already on the blasting table.

"What's this?" I asked, picking it up. It weighed next to nothing.

"My present," said Michael.

"An empty box?"

"No," he laughed. "There's a photo inside."

"Of?" I persisted. Michael blushed.

"C'mon!" I said, nudging him with my shoulder. "Tell Brett. What's inside the itty bitty boxie?" Deeper blush. This had to be good. I leaned toward Michael and spoke quietly into his ear.

"I'll tell you mine if you tell me yours." I couldn't believe I was teasing him this way, but I couldn't make myself stop.

"Hands!" he burst out, surprising us both.

"Huh?" I asked.

"A picture of my hands. I want to get rid of my nail biting, so I'm blasting a picture of my hands."

"Oh. Cool," I replied, somehow disappointed. I don't know what I expected. It was actually a fine intention. Michael's worst, not-so-gifted talent is chewing his nails down to painful stubs.

"So tell me yours," he said. I hesitated.

"Actually . . . I haven't decided yet what to blast."

"Cheater!" he exclaimed. "You know. Spill it."

"Come inside for a minute," I sighed. "I still haven't wrapped it." Michael followed me upstairs to where I had hidden my gift in Nonna's spare bedroom.

"Guess," I said, pulling it from a brown paper bag and holding it up.

Considering how good my mom is with her hands, it's amazing how utterly hopeless I am with crafty projects. My gift was a monumental flop. I had started with a wire coat hanger, bent it to the shape I wanted, packed it with paper, then wrapped strips of glue-soaked newsprint over it. When it dried, I painted it bright red. Unfortunately, it didn't hold its shape, and the paint cracked and flaked.

Michael narrowed his eyes. I could hear the gears in his brain creak under the weight of this impossible question.

"A bloody snake eating its own tail? Harry, it's the Dark Mark!" he squealed in a girlish British accent.

I sighed, tossing the papier-mâché mess on the bed.

"Skip the Hermione Granger imitation, okay? It's supposed to be a mouth. See, these are red lips."

Michael picked it up. "A mouth," he repeated thoughtfully, turning it over in his hands.

"A big mouth," I explained. "My big fat uncontrollable mouth. I came up with the idea after . . . after you got mad at me. You know?" Michael continued to turn my mouth over in his hands.

"It's like, stuff just comes out of my mouth. And lately it

seems like everything I say is wrong and makes people mad. Or hurts people's feelings. And that day—with you—I realized how much better off I'd be without my stupid mouth. Saying stupid things."

Michael placed the mouth gently on the bed. "It's okay," he said quietly.

"I'm really sorry, Michael."

"It's okay," he repeated, and smiled. I felt like one-ton weights had been cut from my legs and I could soar heavenward, like a hot-air balloon.

Just then we heard a car pulling into the drive and heard my father call to Nonna.

"Mother! Someone's here. What time did you tell everyone to arrive?"

"I didn't, actually," she called from inside the house. In the garage, where she was screwing cans of propane onto the Coleman stoves, my mother said something I would have gotten punished for repeating. Michael and I exchanged shocked grins.

"Time to party," I said.

ma·ca·bre

I don't know what came faster: snow or guests. As it turns out, the McCarthys were ready for neither.

But as that turns out, it didn't matter.

Five members of Elders United for Peace and Social Justice arrived in that first car. "Hope we're not too early!" they called out to Nonna, who waited for them at the front door. Locking elbows and stepping carefully along the unshoveled walkway, they all spoke at once.

"None of us drives at night, so we figured we'd come now!" "How about this snow! We're supposed to get eight inches." "Put us to work, Eileen!"

Here's the thing about Nonna's friends: They're the dig-in types. *What* they dig into varies. Some garden, so they dig. Literally. Others are really political, so they argue. Constantly. The Elders are emphatically peaceful, social, and just. The hikers have trekked thousands of miles, the book groupies read so voraciously that local librarians complain that they don't know what to recommend for them anymore. Whatever the group, whatever the cause, they do it with gusto.

Mom's extremely annoyed expression changed to relief as more of Nonna's busy-bee friends pulled up in their cars and rolled up their sleeves. And before all 123 guests had arrived, the bonfires blazed, hot drinks steamed on the outdoor stoves, lights twinkled throughout the yard, and the bazooka blasted.

The Gnome Home filled to bursting. I overheard a friend of Dad's remark he hadn't attended such a loud, crowded event since his last college frat party. Outside, packs of children in snowsuits frisked like puppies in the snow. Wired on chocolate desserts, they screamed and ran in aimless circles. Blasts from the bazooka only served to rev them up even more.

Here's how it worked.

Arriving guests would make their way through the packed house to where Nonna sat in the living room. They'd hug, say the usual Happy Birthday thing, then present her with their blasting item.

The range of gifts varied. For example, the Lighthearted: "Here are a gazillion plastic McDonald's Happy Meal toys I keep meaning to throw out!"

The Serious: "Here are my cigarettes. I'm finally going to quit!"

The Revealing: "Here are two tickets to the racetrack. I'm going to stop betting on the horses!"

The Just Plain Stupid: "Here's a picture of Usher. He thinks he's so cool, but he's not!"

Nonna loved them all, thanked everyone enthusiastically, and handed each item to me: the Runner. I'd dart outside to where Michael and Mr. Beady manned the bazooka and pass whatever it was to them. Mr. Beady had gotten hold of an air horn for the evening, and before stuffing each gift into the PVC pipe, he'd make an announcement.

"Attention! Now firing Mrs. Blakely's check register! She says she hasn't balanced the checkbook in ten months and has decided to give up altogether!" Everyone stopped what they were doing for a moment to observe the blast, cheered as Michael fired the bazooka, and applauded wildly when bits of burned paper floated to the ground. Everyone except Mr. Blakely, now that I think of it.

It went on like this all evening: lots of eating, socializing, playing. Intermittently interrupted by a blast.

I was having a good time, despite my obsessive need to keep checking the front door. Finally, there was a ring I could hear over all the loud laughter and chatter, and when I answered it, she was there. She'd come with her mother and Merrill.

"Hey," I said, smiling. "You made it."

"Hello, Brett! Of course we made it! We wouldn't have missed it for the world!" Mrs. Pelletier exclaimed, throwing her arms around my neck and startling me with a big happy hug. She seemed electrically enthusiastic.

"Where is your grandmother? Oh . . . never mind! I see her. Oh . . . she looks wonderful! Doesn't she? Isn't she wonderful? I have to say hello." Mrs. Pelletier released her hold on me and pushed through the crowd toward Nonna.

"My mother doesn't get out much these days," Diane said, a trace of apology in her voice. "She works practically all the time."

"She takes Paxil," Merrill piped up.

"What?" I said.

"Merrill . . . shut up," Diane snapped.

"Happy pills," he continued, undeterred by the menace in his sister's voice. "She used to cry all the time, but now she takes Paxil and she's happy again." I looked at Diane.

"I'm sorry," she said, shaking her head. "I'm sure you're not interested in hearing the sad story of the Pelletier family. And Merrill . . ." She directed her gaze at her little brother. "That's Mommy's private business. Don't go telling people Mommy's business."

Merrill looked puzzled. "But it's *Brett*," he said. Brett isn't "people" is what he meant. Brett's your best friend. Right?

"Do you want to say hi to Nonna?" I asked him, trying to change the subject. "She'll be really glad you came."

"Yes, I want to show her what I brought," he said seriously.

"What did you bring?" I asked, a few ideas floating through my head. Those waxy fake vampire teeth he kept popping in and out of his mouth one Halloween? Samples from his dead-bug collection? I hadn't stepped foot inside the Pelletiers' for months, but I could still picture Merrill's messy room and its little-boy contents.

"Blankie," he said.

This stopped me in my tracks. "Did you say 'blankie'?" I asked. He nodded.

The only thing Merrill Pelletier cared about more than television was his blankie. His intense attachment to his horrible, nappy rag of a blanket rivaled that of Linus, from the Peanuts gang. I had often suspected Merrill loved blankie more than he loved his own mother.

"Merrill, do you realize what Nonna's going to do with blankie?" I asked him.

"She's going to fire it from the bazooka," he said. "That's okay. Remember, I saw the bazooka at the garage sale?"

"I know, but Merrill, blankie won't survive. The bazooka will ruin it." Torch it, I thought.

"That's okay," he said again, a bit insistently.

"We've tried talking to him, but it's pointless," Diane said, shrugging. She seemed indifferent.

"Okay," I sighed. If his own sister would let him do this, who was I to interfere?

We found Mrs. Pelletier with Nonna. She was remarking, loudly, how gorgeous Nonna's cap looked.

From the beginning, Nonna had refused wigs. "It's one thing to look bald, another to look macabre. I won't do it," she'd said.

Macabre: *tending to produce horror in a beholder.* Scary.

At first, when she still had a bit of hair, Nonna just went with it. But now that the cold weather had set in, she covered up. Sometimes with soft scarves but more often with cotton caps. The one she wore this night was a Brett McCarthy special, knit on circular needles. I'd called it an island cap and chosen colors that reminded us of Spruce Island: light blue, like the sky on a clear day; balsam green, for the trees; and purple, for the eggplants Nonna always tried—and failed—to grow in her garden. The cap came out hopelessly lumpy, but Nonna loved it anyway.

"I can't believe you *made* it, Brett! It's just wonderful! I didn't know you could knit! But of course, your mother is so creative. All of you McCarthys . . . so creative! Diane, did you see this? Look what Brett made!" Mrs. Pelletier enthused.

"Cool," Diane said politely.

I could feel myself missing the old Brett-banning Mrs. Pelletier. Paxil Pelletier was making me nervous.

"Honey, it's great to see you." Nonna had taken Diane's hand and smiled warmly at her. I watched Diane to see if she registered any surprise. Nonna had changed dramatically over the past months. Gone from wrinkly and robust to pale and birdlike thin. It shocked people who hadn't seen her much.

Diane didn't miss a beat.

"I'm really happy you invited us, Nonna," she said sincerely. "Happy birthday."

"Happy birthday!" Merrill exclaimed, pushing a brown paper bag into Nonna's lap.

"Oh, thank you, Merrill," Nonna laughed. "Let's see what's in here." She reached in and pulled out a gray, tattered cloth.

"Hmm," Nonna said. "You know . . . I think I know what this is." She frowned.

"Can you believe it?" Mrs. Pelletier laughed. Not quite hysterically, but close. "He says *this* is what he wants to get rid of!"

"I'm a big boy," Merrill said quietly.

"Excuse me?" Nonna asked.

"I said I'm a big boy now," Merrill repeated, louder. "Big boys don't have blankies."

Nonna looked carefully at Merrill. Peering at him with her X-ray vision, straight into his heart. I'd seen that look a zillion times before, aimed at me.

"I have to," he whispered to her. "I have to be big."

Nonna nodded at him, patted his arm, and stuffed blankie back into the bag. She handed it to me.

"You're absolutely right," she said. "Do you want to go outside and help Beady blast blankie?"

"And Diane's too," Merrill said.

"Diane's blasting a blankie?" Nonna said.

"Oh, no," Diane said, handing Nonna a white, folded cloth she'd been holding since they'd arrived. "I want to get rid of this old T-shirt. My drawers are full of clothes I've outgrown."

"You know . . . I saw you walk in that door and thought you looked taller!" Nonna said.

"Can you believe it?" Mrs. Pelletier gushed. "She's grown an inch and gained five pounds since the fall! Pretty soon my little girl is going to be taller than me! They grow up so fast. Where does the time go?"

A little twitch at the corner of Diane's mouth was my first indication that she'd finally had it with her mother. I think the five pounds did it. As opposed to me—I gain or lose five pounds any given weekend depending on how much chocolate I can get my hands on—Diane keeps tight control on her eating.

"Ready to go outside and blast?" I offered. Clearly relieved, Diane nodded. We headed out, with Merrill close behind.

The night air was perfectly cold. Perfect, because it was cold enough to keep the snow powdery, but not so cold that your fingers ached or your toes grew numb. Merrill dashed ahead of us toward Mr. Beady and Michael, toting the paper bag with blankie and the T-shirt. Diane and I followed, awkwardly silent. Suddenly she stopped.

"Do you know what this is?" she asked, looking all around.

"What?" I said.

"Angel snow," she said. "Look."

About a dozen feet away from us glittered smooth, untrammeled snow the kids had missed. Upon its surface the moon reflected crystals, diamonds, and bright points of light. When we were little girls, we would go out at night in search of such snow. We'd stand at the edge of a patch, arms outspread, and fall back flat. Then, with legs and arms madly brushing up and down, we'd make Diane and Brett angels. The trick was getting up without sticking your hand through a wing or your boot through a gown.

I held my arms out, sideways, and grinned at her.

"Do it!" I cried, falling back. Diane giggled, and within seconds the two of us were on our backs in the snow. I could feel icy crystals on my neck and snow in my hair. We flapped our arms and legs in horizontal jumping jacks, creating long choir-robe sleeves and flowing dresses. When we'd flapped enough, we lay still. It was oddly peaceful. The commotion from the party seemed miles away, and Mr. Beady appeared to have taken a break from the bazooka blasting. We stared silently together at the winter stars overhead.

"I'm sorry about my mom," I heard Diane say. "She's hard to take these days."

"You don't have to apologize," I said to the moon overhead. "She probably can't help it."

"It sure beats the way she was right after Dad moved out," Diane continued. "She was a mess. If she wasn't crying, she was yelling. Finally she got her doctor to prescribe something. But it's made her . . . almost *too* happy, you know?"

"Maniacally happy?" I suggested.

"Exactly." Diane laughed. "You always come up with just the right word, Brett."

There was a pause as we both absorbed the effect of this compliment.

"Actually, I don't," I finally said.

"What do you mean?"

I took a deep breath.

"I didn't have the right words when your Dad moved out. I blew you off even though Kit told me what had happened. That was bad."

"Yeah, it was," Diane said quietly.

"I was mad that you didn't tell me about the cheerleading, you know?"

Silence.

"I was also mad when I saw you with Jeanne Anne. You know, that day after we made the phone call?"

"The day you hit her," Diane added.

"It was—she wrecked my life, and there you were talking to her. About me."

"We were talking about *Bob*," Diane said. "We were talking about the whole thing at the water fountain."

"*And* me," I added.

"Of course," Diane replied. "But we weren't being mean."

"Maybe *you* weren't, but she can't help herself," I said.

Diane sighed. "Okay, sometimes she's mean. But she's also really funny, you know? You never cut her any slack."

"All right . . . you know . . . I don't want to talk about Jeanne Anne. It gets my adrenaline going. I'm sorry I brought it up."

We didn't speak for a few minutes.

"You know why I didn't tell you about the cheerleading?" Diane whispered.

"Why?"

"I knew it would make you mad."

"No, it made me mad when I thought you were keeping secrets from me. You could have told me."

"Brett . . . please." Diane had a give-me-a-break tone in her voice. "You hate cheerleading and you are a very opinionated person and you would have made me feel terrible for trying out. And you know what? I *wanted* to try out. I'm *glad* I made it. It's loads of fun, and if I were still your friend, I wouldn't have even tried."

Still your friend. Those words hung in the air. Like icicles suspended from a branch. Diane had said it so matter-of-factly.

"So . . . we're not friends anymore?" Even I could tell how pathetic the question sounded.

"Well, what do you think?" Diane replied. "I mean, no offense, but I've moved on."

"Moved on. Like, with Bob?"

"No, not just with *Bob*. With everything. With different interests, different people. I mean, I think we've outgrown each other, don't you?"

I couldn't believe her words. I couldn't believe how utterly clueless I had been. Here I was, assuming that whatever had gone wrong between Diane and me could be fixed. A few apologies and we'd be right back where we'd started. Right?

Not right.

It occurred to me that Diane had to have learned this somewhere. Unfortunately, I put my thoughts to words.

"Is that what your dad told your mom?" I said. "That he'd outgrown her? That he'd moved on?"

Big mouth. Brett McCarthy: Violent, Suspended, Practically Friendless, Biggest Big Mouth in the Eighth Grade. Not that I was wrong, mind you. But I didn't need to say it.

Diane stood up. She made two big boot prints in the middle of her angel.

"And you think Jeanne Anne's mean?" she said quietly. "You don't know anything—*anything*—about my family. Or me."

I scrambled up from the snow, trashing my angel as well. "I'm sorry," I said. "It's like I told you. I'm *not* good with words. I use the wrong ones all the time. Do you know, I made a papier-mâché mouth for this party tonight? That's what I want to blast from the bazooka: my big mouth."

Diane was listening to me with her arms folded across her chest. Not very promising body language.

"I don't know what you're talking about, and I don't think I care. I'm outta here." She turned and began retracing our footprints back to the house. I decided to make one last try.

"You're wrong!" I said. "I do know you. Better than Jeanne Anne. Better than Darcy. Or Bob, even. And you're not like them, Diane."

She interrupted her retreat to the house and turned to face me.

"What you don't seem to *get*," she finally said, "is that I'm not like *you*."

sur·re·al

By midnight only the Emergency Contacts remained: Aunt Lorena and Uncle Jack (with Michael, of course) and Mr. Beady. They helped Mom and Dad deal with the post-party wreckage. Brownies mashed into the carpet. Crushed paper cups sticking out of the snow. Junk littered across the lawn from the blastings.

Until the last guest had left, Nonna remained in her armchair by the window, regally receiving gifts and greetings and watching from the comfort of her warm house. Now, party over, she finally got up.

"Eileen, don't even think of cleaning," Mom said. She was on her knees under the kitchen table, picking up spent birthday candles.

The highlight of the evening had been the brownie lighting. More than a hundred people, packed elbow to elbow inside the overheated house, or outside, encircling the bonfire dishes, held paper plates with little flickering lights and sang to Nonna. As one, we'd each blown out our candle and made a wish, and for a second there was absolute quiet. No one spoke as all our silent wishes floated up to the stars. Then everybody cheered.

"No, no," Nonna said to Mom. "This girl knows her limits. But I do want Brett to help me outside. Just for a minute."

This, it turns out, was no small task. It took a lot of layers to get Nonna warm enough to leave the house, especially at night.

"You look like the Michelin Man," I commented as I zipped her parka. In addition to a turtleneck, sweater, and fleece vest, she wore long johns, sweats, and Mom's ski pants.

"Why, thank you," she said. "Grab that bag." She pointed to a canvas tote near her armchair.

"Remind me what we're doing?" I asked.

"Last blasts," she said.

I had forgotten all about my gift. Diane was on my mind. After our "conversation," she'd returned to the Gnome Home, pulled her mother aside, and whispered into her ear. Mrs. Pelletier had looked confused, but within minutes she had said goodbye to Nonna, packed Merrill and Diane into the car, and driven off.

I had seen this all from outside, standing alongside the trampled snow angels and watching it play out behind the picture window. It was surreal.

Surreal: *having the intense irrational reality of a dream.* Like when Jeanne Anne placed that call to Bob. Like watching an ambulance pull up your driveway. You have this uncontrollable desire to turn back time, rewind, return to normal.

I felt regret, no doubt about it. But another part of me felt . . . relief. The truth was out: Diane Pelletier was not my best friend. Hadn't been for a while, only the Queen of Denial had been too obtuse to realize it. Our friendship had been redefining itself since . . . I don't know . . . the beginning of junior high? So while it *seemed* like some single event—a prank phone call, a divorce, a sick grandmother—had pushed us apart, it was a lot more complicated and more gradual than that.

And here's the really surprising part: It was okay. It was sad, but in the world of Big Bad Redefining Things, this was manageable. Diane was right: I wasn't like her. And while that didn't matter when we were very little girls, it did now. Especially because our differences had to do with people. She chose Jeanne Anne and the Darcy crowd. I chose Michael and Kit and the Fifth Period gang. We were worlds apart.

Michael was shaking a can of Aqua Net and Mr. Beady was waiting patiently as Nonna and I approached.

"Eileen, I do believe if you hit the ground, you'll bounce," he said.

"That's always been a personal goal of mine," Nonna declared, "but perhaps we can put it off for another evening. Right now, Beady, I want to see what you've got for me."

Mr. Beady cleared his throat dramatically and reached into a deep inner pocket of his winter coat. He pulled out a paperback book. Opening it to a page he had folded, he began to read.

" 'What do they think has happened, the old fools, / To make them like this?' " he began. He did not get one word further. Nonna clapped her hands over her eyes and shook her head.

"No, not Philip Larkin!" she cried. "No no *no* Beady, he's all wrong!"

"Once I might have disagreed with you, but not anymore," Mr. Beady declared. "Eileen, I have finally come to your way of thinking about Philip Larkin, and tonight, as a special gift to you, I am going blast my copy of his collected works."

"Do you have any idea what they are talking about?" Michael muttered to me.

"Sort of," I replied. "I'll tell you later."

"So, now, Philip Larkin, to borrow from the words of Eileen's *favorite poet*, Dylan Thomas, I bid you to go not gentle but *loudly* into this good night!" Mr. Beady proclaimed. He stuffed the book down the PVC pipe, squirted some hair spray into the base, and pressed the ignition key. *Poof!* The collected works shot from the pipe, and with a soft *swoosh* the sheets of glowing, singed papers floated back down to earth. Nonna beat her heavily mittened hands together hard.

"Beady, it takes a great man to admit he's wrong," Nonna said.

"Then I must be very great, because I am often wrong," he

replied, putting his arm around Nonna's shoulders. "Except about you. Happy birthday, my dear, dear friend." Nonna rested her head on Mr. Beady's shoulder.

"Okay, who's next?" Michael asked abruptly. "I think Brett still hasn't gone." I reached into Nonna's tote and pulled out my papier-mâché mess. Leaves of red paint flaked off, dotting the snow.

"Well, if you use your imaginations, you can see that this is a mouth," I explained.

"We don't have that much imagination," Michael said.

"Shut up," I said. "Okay . . . this is a mouth. And as you all probably know, my big mouth has gotten me in a lot of trouble lately. More lately than you even realize. I think it's something I need to get rid of." I handed the mouth to Mr. Beady, who accepted it solemnly.

"Go on, Mr. Beady. Blast it," I said. Mr. Beady stuffed, sprayed, and ignited, and my big mouth shot over the woods like a falling star. Nonna squeezed my shoulders and planted a soft kiss on my cold cheek.

"Michael's already gone, so that leaves just me," Nonna said.

"Why are you blasting? It's *your* birthday!" I said.

"This is my gift to myself," Nonna replied. She reached into the tote and pulled out a medium-sized Nalgene bottle.

"You're getting rid of a water bottle?" Michael asked.

"No, it's just a receptacle," Nonna explained. "There's

something inside. But even though I need to lose it, I couldn't bear to burn it in the bazooka, so I put it in this Nalgene. They're practically indestructible, you know."

"So what is it?" I asked.

"A secret," she said. This caught me up short.

"Seriously. What are you blasting?" It never occurred to me that she wouldn't answer.

"I'm not going to tell you, Brett," she said firmly. "It's private. Please respect that." She handed the Nalgene to Mr. Beady.

Mr. Beady solemnly held the bottle over the mouth of the pipe for a moment before letting it slide down. I could see a white envelope stuffed inside.

"Three, two, one, fire!" Mr. Beady cried, and the Nalgene exploded from the pipe. The three of them whistled and clapped.

"And now, ladies—actually, lady—and gentlemen," Nonna declared, "I am long overdue for my beauty sleep. Thank you very, very much for all your blasting efforts at this wonderful party." She took my arm, and we headed slowly back to the Gnome Home. We didn't speak. I think she was too tired to talk. I simply couldn't.

I waited. I waited until the last brownie pan was scrubbed, dried, and put back in the cabinets, the last crushed candle scraped from the carpet. I waited until the taillights of Aunt Lorena and Uncle Jack's car had disappeared down the dark driveway. Until Mr. Beady had dragged the bazooka into the garage and pulled the door shut. I waited as Mom and Dad got Nonna settled down for the night, turned off the Gnome Home kitchen lights, and walked with me across the snowy, glistening lawn to our house.

I waited for them to stop talking quietly in their bedroom, for the light beneath the crack of their door to go out. I waited for Dad's heavy, rhythmic breathing, signaling sleep. Then I crept down the stairs, slipped into my boots and parka, and grabbed a flashlight.

There was a lot of stuff scattered in the snow—blasted bits of paper and cloth—but I knew the object I sought would be intact. Nalgenes can take a beating.

It had traveled far, halfway to the woods. It stuck upright in the snow and didn't even look singed. The top unscrewed easily, and I pulled out the envelope.

It contained a single photograph, one I knew well. Nonna usually kept it on her fridge. It had been taken this past August, from our boat, the *Dolly Llama*. Nonna had clicked the photo as the *Dolly*, piloted by Mr. Beady, buzzed across the water toward Spruce Island. Mom, Dad, and I were on the shore, watching their approach. It was a brilliant summer weekend, one of those bright Maine weekends when every color burns intensely. Like the colors in the cap I'd knitted.

The resulting picture contained the island, the lighthouse tower in the background, and in one small corner the three of us, waving. The things Nonna would have to give up.

I don't know how long I sat there, in the snow, holding the

picture and the Nalgene and rocking back and forth, back and forth, feeling sadder than I ever thought I could possibly feel. And thinking, I'm never going to get up. I'm going to sit here and it's always and forever going to be night and cold.

But after a while I realized my face was wet and swollen. And I was freezing. So of course I went inside. I brought the Nalgene and picture with me. And I put them inside my closet, on the floor, behind boxes of old shoes.

ir•ra•tion•al

Here's the thing about lunch in junior high: It's the Inferno.

What might appear innocently enough as a friendly cafeteria filled with tables is actually Hell, all set out like a giant banquet. Instead of growing boys and girls intent on filling their bellies with wholesome things, we're obsessing about the social order. Choose your dining companions and take your place in the world. It's as simple—and as awful—as that.

Since Suspension #2, I hadn't eaten in the cafeteria. First there were the No-Hare lunch dates. Then, with the introduction of the lighthouse project, the whole Special Challenges class started eating a "working lunch" together in the classroom. Nonna, accompanied by Mr. Beady (he had become her designated driver at that point), joined us on her nonsick days. I don't have to tell you how popular I got with the Fifth Period crowd when my grandmother started showing up with Super-Sized Raspberry Chunk Brownies.

One cold afternoon in January Mrs. Augmentino was

absent and the "working lunch" canceled. So for the first time in months I found myself standing with a loaded tray in a noisy cafeteria, wondering where to sit.

I scanned the room for Kit. She usually ate with Girl Jocks, although she often floated to other tables. She played sax for the jazz ensemble, so sometimes she found herself seated at the Band Table. Occasionally she even joined Diane in Cheerleader World. She called those her "hungry days" and explained that she could pick up whole, uneaten sandwiches from Darcy and Co. "Those girls just don't eat!" she'd say in amazement. But I knew it wasn't really about food.

Kit resisted the clique thing. Even when we were a clique—me, Diane, Kit, and Jeanne Anne—she'd do stuff with other people, even guys, like go to the movies or spend a day at the beach.

"Kit defies the social box," Michael said. I remembered the admiration in his voice when he'd said that. It was the reason he'd moved her from Eat More Than Their Share in the Inferno to True Friends and People Who Are Honest in the Paradiso, Dante's version of Heaven.

He didn't say it, but I suspected it was the reason he'd kept me out of that ring. My inability to get beyond the "social box."

My eyes flitted from group to group, but I couldn't find Kit anywhere. I had just decided to make my way to Girl Jocks when someone nudged me from behind: Monique Rose.

"Hey," she said, pointing across the room. "We're by the

windows." The entire Special Challenges class had taken up the long, sunny table near the windows. There were plenty of empty seats. Monique Rose walked toward them, and I followed.

I put my tray down between Michael and History Dude, right across from Carla Lonsdorf, the Unit. Carla is the slowest slow grower in the school. She barely tops four feet, and she is so thin that her friends have declared her a unit of measure, like a pound. Or an ounce. For example, a car might weigh 65 Carlas. Darcy Dodson probably weighs 1.5 Carlas. Big Joan probably tipped the scale at just under three Carlas.

The Unit's eyes, already enormous behind her thick glasses, widened to owl proportions when she saw my tray. I had two large Oakhurst Dairy milks—a strawberry and a chocolate—in addition to a very full plate of spaghetti.

"Lucky," she said. "My mom won't let me drink flavored milk. She says there's too much sugar."

"She's right," I said, unscrewing the top of the strawberry. "But how would she know if you drink it at school?"

"She gets a weekly printout of everything I've bought for lunch." Carla shrugged. My eyes rested on the colorful salad arranged on her tray.

I chugged about half the milk and held the rest out to her. "You didn't buy this one."

Before she could reply, a familiar voice cut into our conversation.

"Check it out. Look who's sitting with the Nerd Herd."

It had been a long time since Darcy and Co. had bothered

to taunt me. I assumed I had fallen so low in the social order that it wasn't worth their effort. Mocking McCarthy had gotten too easy, like shooting fish in a barrel. But sitting with the Fifth Period gang was a not-to-be-missed opportunity. Especially for Jeanne Anne, walking by with Darcy and just within earshot of a table packed with Demigods.

"Hey, Brett, no offense, but you're not smart enough to sit with the Herd," Jeanne Anne said. "Although . . . you are *desperate* enough!" Darcy's high-pitched laughter followed. I looked across the table and saw two bright patches of red appear on the Unit's cheeks. To my right, Michael was staring at his plate as if it were the most fascinating thing in the world.

I stood up, fast. There's something about standing up swiftly in a crowded junior high cafeteria. You get people's attention, especially if they've come to expect irrational behavior from you.

Irrational: *lacking usual or normal mental clarity or coherence.* Acting in a way that could lead to suspension.

My hands closed. I tried to pick from one of the really choice comments forming in my mind. Violent, Practically Friendless, Juvenile Delinquent, Redefined Brett McCarthy took a deep breath and—

"Oh. My. God!" I said this loudly, with feeling. I looked, with exaggerated panic, at Jeanne Anne, then at the kids sitting at my table. I knew I had an audience. "Are you saying that these people are . . . are . . . NERDS?!?" I clapped my hand over my mouth in horror. I widened my eyes. Poor Carla looked terrified. Michael had his arms folded across his chest, a puzzled frown on his face.

"Jeanne Anne, Jeanne Anne, I had no idea!" I exclaimed. "I thought they were BRAINS! That's what they told me! I had no idea they were . . . NERDS!" Someone snickered behind us. A Demigod.

"Hey," said a kid sitting left of History Dude. "Who are you calling a Nerd? I'm a Geek, and proud of it."

"Well, speak for yourself, Geek," said Michael. He stood up. "I'm an Einstein." He looked at me. I caught the trace of a grin.

A hand shot up. A friend of Michael's from math team who looked like a walking Fifth Period cliché, with short pants, white socks, and a piece of tape holding his glasses together. "I'm an Einstein too," he said.

"Hey, man, I'm Einstein Three!" boomed a voice from Boy Jocks, followed by deep laughs and some table pounding. Whoops of laughter now.

"Excuse me!" The Unit stood. Her cheeks were still pink, but she'd lost the panicked look. She faced Jeanne Anne. "I am not a Geek. I'm Gifted, thank you." She sat down again. She picked up my strawberry milk and took a long gulp.

I threw my arms around Jeanne Anne's shoulders and gave her a not-so-friendly squeeze.

"Thanks for warning me, Jeanne Anne, but it's okay. See, they're not Nerds after all."

She pushed me off, glaring. She looked like a cat ready to spit.

"You are such a loser, McCarthy," she said angrily. "Don't touch me."

I closed my eyes, pressed my hands against my chest, and fell back with a theatrical faint.

"A loser! She called me a loser!" I exclaimed loudly. "My heart is broken. Does that mean it's all over between us, honey? Please, don't be mad at me!"

Jeanne Anne walked quickly away, toward a section of table where Darcy was already seated. Low whistles and a few kissy noises from the Demigods followed her. "Hey, honey, don't get mad!" one of them crooned. "C'mon, let's make up!" I had a feeling Jeanne Anne would be sure to stay as far away as possible from me in the future.

Meanwhile, high fives were being exchanged down the length of the Special Challenges table. Broken Glasses Kid was arguing with Michael that actually *he* should be Einstein One, since he'd scored three points higher in their latest Math Olympiad. Carla was polishing off the last of my strawberry milk. Michael just had this very—I don't know— self-satisfied look on his face. Like he had a secret.

When the bell rang and everyone drifted toward the exit doors, he and I walked out together, not talking. Just heading to the lockers like nobody's business. Einstein and Brett McCarthy, Class Clown.

om·ni·pres·ent

The Lighthouse Project turned out to be one of the biggest genius turn-ons in Special Challenges history. Even the ever-delighted Mrs. Augmentino had no words to describe her amazement at what Fifth Period produced. The range of projects prompted her to ask No-Hare to create Lighthouse Day and invite the entire student body to see what we'd made.

All the McCarthys, plus the omnipresent Mr. Beady, planned to attend.

Omnipresent: *always there.*

He'd found an all-terrain wheelchair, equipped with fat snow tires, just for the occasion. At that point, the deepest, coldest part of winter, Nonna was moving slowly, and preventing her from slipping on ice had become a major family preoccupation. My mother must have purchased forty bags of rock salt from Wal-Mart and coated the Gnome Home front walk and driveway a full inch deep. Dad had bought Nonna these lightweight winter hiking shoes from L.L.Bean and was trying to convince her to wear them indoors as well as out.

"I'm just walking to the bathroom! Not climbing Everest!" she'd complained when he'd presented them to her. She seemed deaf to his explanations about the dangers of soft socks on wood floors.

"Eileen, please," Mom had said. "If you fall and break a hip, it's all over."

Nonna wore the hikers. She wore my island cap, a fun fur scarf, and her Michelin Man parka. She wore her lined wool cross-country ski pants and scarlet Hot Chilis insulated socks. And when Mr. Beady wheeled her into the Fifth Period classroom dressed like that on Lighthouse Day, you'd have thought J.Lo had just stepped onto the red carpet. We'd been milling around, admiring all the projects displayed on tables and on the walls of the classroom, when we heard an excited "She's here!" Someone clapped, and as my family entered, the whole group applauded.

Mrs. Augmentino had set aside the first half hour as a little party just for Fifth Period and invited guests. Mrs. LaVoie was there. So was my former lunch buddy and fellow Tar Heels fan, No-Hare. The cafeteria provided a big plastic bowl of red punch, and I provided McCarthyesque Super-Sized sweets. Monique Rose and the Unit had come over the night before to bake with me.

"Why are you cutting them so big?" Carla had asked. The

fact that I was slicing only six brownies to the pan really worried her.

"It's what they do," Monique Rose explained.

" 'They'?" I asked.

"You and your grandmother," she said to me. "These big desserts. It's sort of your signature characteristic. You had them at the birthday party. You always do them at your garage sale."

"You've been to the garage sale?" I asked, surprised.

"Every year," she said.

"I've never seen you," I said, amazed. "Where have you been hiding?"

"Where have you been looking?" Monique Rose asked.

Standing alongside her, next to our trifold display "Maine Island Stories," I was struck anew how strange it was that someone who'd previously existed on another planet could suddenly be my project partner, lunch companion, and describer of McCarthy family "signature characteristics." I knew it was odd for her too. One afternoon, when we were walking to the Gnome Home together after school, she'd blurted out, "I still can't get over that we're friends, you know? I always thought you were some brainless jock."

The word hung in the air, like the frost from our breath: friends. Violent, Suspended, Redefined Me had actually managed to *make* a friend, as opposed to *losing* one.

"Yeah, well, don't kid yourself," I'd said. "I *am* a brainless jock."

Mr. Beady, Nonna, Mom, and Dad began their circuit of the room with us.

"Fairy houses!" Mom exclaimed. Monique Rose had suggested we construct a little fairy village of twigs, moss, pinecones, and stones to display before our trifold. They went with the island stories about ghosts and pixies, although Monique Rose had learned that *those* stories were often cooked up by islanders trying to scare or intimidate their neighbors.

Nonna leaned over, peering into the front door of a fairy house.

"It makes me wish I were thimble-sized and could lie on a little moss bed," she said.

"Beautiful work, hon," Mom said, looking over our trifold. "I love the way you've woven interviews and family anecdotes into old stories and history."

"You weave with fibers; Brett weaves with words," Mr. Beady said proudly. I looked at him, surprised. It had never occurred to me that Mr. Beady had any pride of ownership in me. Nonna twisted around in the wheelchair to look up at him.

"Have you noticed that ever since you blasted Philip Larkin, you've become wise and insightful?"

"Yes, yes," he said, patting her shoulder and shaking his head. I could tell he was sorry he'd ever heard the name Philip Larkin.

Mom's eyes had filled. "Remember all the fairy houses we used to make?" she said.

"We can still make them," I said quickly. "I still love to make them."

"You're never too old to make fairy houses," Nonna agreed. Mom smiled at me, and I gave her one back before they wheeled off to the final, climactic portion of the classroom. The lights.

Although most kids stuck to the assignment and tried to re-create a lighthouse from 1803, a few of them decided to simply let their genius imaginations run wild. In one corner of the room a couple of boys were torching a pile of sticks atop a little rock tower: That was the Egyptian lighthouse, modeled after one of the Seven Wonders of the Ancient World. Interesting and certainly smoky, but not relevant. Near the window a kid had put together a laser light powered by these little solar panels, which also fueled tiny lead-acid batteries. This project would probably gain him early acceptance to Harvard someday, but it wasn't the Jeffersonian solution we wanted.

Michael had done it. He'd figured out that Spruce Island light had been commissioned just about when Lewis and Clark were exploring the Louisiana Purchase. He researched the sorts of lamps used at the time and discovered that Argand lamps—which used concave reflectors and glass cylinders around the wick—didn't make it to the United States until 1813. So his hunch was that Spruce Island was first lit with whale-oil-burning lanterns. His "light" was nothing more than sixteen kerosene (he couldn't get whale oil without committing a serious crime) lanterns arranged in a circle with flat tin-and-mirror reflectors behind them.

"How simple!" Nonna exclaimed. "All this time I've been thinking we had to construct some complicated crystal thingie . . . but this is all it took. Amazing."

"The trick will be setting it up," Dad said. "That tower needs a lot of work."

"You know, that brings me to something I've been meaning to ask all of you," said Mrs. Augmentino. The whole class quieted.

"The students have heard so much about your island from Brett, and become so *very* involved in this project, that we wondered . . . might the class take a trip out to Spruce Island once the light is installed? It would be a *marvelous* way to wrap up the year!"

Something clutched in my chest. My mind fast-forwarded to warm months in late June, our family boat, the *Dolly Llama*, laden with waterproof wet bags and food-filled coolers, plowing through blue waves that mirrored the sky. These were images I often hugged to myself, like a cozy fleece blanket, during the dark winter months. But time didn't feel like a friend anymore. Turning calendar pages seemed dangerous these days.

"Of course!" Nonna exclaimed. "I can't think of a better way to . . . christen the light. Does one christen a light, Beady? Oh, at any rate . . . yes. Absolutely yes."

Cheers, claps, excited chatter. I could hear Monique Rose speaking insistently in my ear about fairy houses, see Mrs.

Augmentino bend over to hug Nonna and enthuse about how incredibly marvelous this had all turned out to be. But the McCarthys just looked sort of numb. Mom held Dad's hand as he examined one of Michael's lanterns like it was the most fascinating thing in the world. Mr. Beady stared at the floor; then, as if he could feel my eyes on him, he looked up at me. And I realized I wasn't the only one in the room who had fantasies about turning back the clock. Or at the very least slowing it down.

per·sist·ent

Early March, a Friday, was one of Nonna's bad nights. By March a bad night meant she couldn't sleep and didn't want to be alone. Later, "bad" would take on a whole new meaning, and we would look back on those cold March nights like they were the good ol' days.

Our definitions of even the simplest words, like "bad" and "good," shifted week to week, changed like the weather, surprised you like a crocus poking from the snow. Hey, you'd think. Winter's gone. That happened fast. But it didn't. It happened slowly, while you thought of other things. And suddenly you faced a whole new season, whole new definitions of good and bad and pain.

Thursday had also been bad, and my parents were tired. So since Friday wasn't a school night, they said I could stay with Nonna. I had my orders: Call us if you need help; don't cook or do anything that would make Nonna get out of bed; don't keep her awake if she can sleep.

I went armed for a slumber party. I brought my iPod because Nonna said listening to music helped her. I brought some videos—she special-requested an oldie called *Casablanca*. I brought Dad's high school yearbook—I liked going through the pictures and encouraging her to tell me inappropriate stories about the kids he grew up with. I brought bananas, one of the few things she still had a taste for.

But nothing worked. Nonna kept twisting on the bed, failing to find a comfortable position. She wouldn't eat, not even the bananas. She couldn't sleep. She didn't want to listen to music and barely paid attention to the boring black-and-white movie (although I managed to watch it all). I had run out of things to say, and we faced the prospect of a long, sleepless wait for dawn. I began to understand why my parents seemed so wrecked.

However, despite my long list of shortcomings, I am nothing if not persistent.

Persistent: *continuing without change in function.* Never giving up.

"Nonna!" I said. "How about a little truth or dare?"

"Hmmm," she said. "I don't know if I can handle any dares at the moment."

Nonna and I played hardball truth or dare. Once she refused to tell me whether Dad had ever gotten into trouble when he was in junior high. So I made her eat an entire jar of peanut butter. Another time (it was January) I refused to reveal if there was a boy at school I had a crush on. She made me wear my bathing suit and run around the outside of the house. Twice.

"Well then, you'll just have to tell the truth," I said.

"You are a heartless creature," she said. "Who goes first?"

"Me." I pulled the armchair I was sitting in up close to her pillow.

"Is Mr. Beady your boyfriend?" I asked her.

None of us had ever spoken about Nonna's relationship with Mr. Beady; not to her, not to each other. Well, maybe Mom and Dad did, but not with me. Mr. Beady was just one of those Facts of Life: Nonna's buddy, always there, smack-dab in the middle of things and utterly undefined. When I was little, I hadn't given it much thought. But these days, it filled me with questions.

Nonna shifted sideways to get a better look at me. She grimaced, and I could tell the movement hurt. But then her expression relaxed.

"He's my best friend," she said. And that was all.

"Yeah, but is he your *boy*friend?" I persisted. "You know. *Boy*friend." I raised my eyebrows suggestively. Nonna laughed.

"He's long past being a boy of any sort," she replied. "So I guess you'd call him a *man*friend. But I'd call him my best. Has been for a long time."

"You're avoiding the question," I said. "I'm gonna make you eat something gross."

"You'll have to wipe it up," she said dryly. "Now tell me what you don't understand."

224

"There are friends, and then there are *friends*," I said. "There are the guys you just hang out with, and then there are the guys . . . you date. Or marry. And since you're not married to Mr. Beady but spend so much time with him, I wondered . . ."

"Oh, I see," she said. "You want to know if we make out?"

"No! Gross!" I exclaimed.

"Why gross?" she asked. "Do you think old people don't make out?"

"Do they?" I asked, incredulous.

"Of course they do," Nonna said, a little impatiently. "Old people do everything young people do. Just more carefully."

This was information I hadn't sought. It wasn't the answer to my question, either, although now the question itself seemed . . . questionable.

"I guess I just don't *get* your relationship with Mr. Beady," I said.

"Well, let me ask you something," Nonna said. "Is Michael your boyfriend?"

"No," I said immediately.

"Why not?" Nonna asked. "He's a boy. He's quite handsome." I made a face. "He thinks the world of you. I'd say he's your best friend."

"But he's not my *boy*friend," I replied.

"Nope," Nonna said, closing her eyes. "I don't buy that for a minute. Head straight into the kitchen, fetch the sardines, and eat the entire tin."

"I'm telling the truth!" I exclaimed.

"You are avoiding the truth," Nonna said. I didn't want to tell her where I'd heard that before.

"Nonna, do you think I make out with Michael? Because I'll tell you: I do not."

"Well, I don't make out with Beady either. Of course, I can scarcely sit up these days, so I'm sure that doesn't surprise you. But don't you think both of our questions miss the point?" she said. I shrugged.

"We don't need to affix some title to Beady or Michael in order to understand what our hearts tell us is so. We don't need to define them with words like 'boyfriend' or 'best friend' or 'lover.' They are dear to us, and we cherish them, and we keep that in mind with every word we say and everything we do." Nonna closed her eyes and sighed deeply.

She was quiet for a long time, and I realized the mere effort of talking exhausted her. I wondered for one hopeful moment if she'd finally fallen asleep, but then she twisted uncomfortably and looked at me with bright, urgent eyes.

"Brett," she said, "in the bathroom cabinet there's a box of fentanyl patches. Bring them in here."

Fentanyl patches had only just entered our vocabulary. Band-Aid–like rectangles about the size of your hand, each contained a twelve-hour dose of pain medication. Nonna had begun to use them on the bad nights. The box I retrieved for her, with directions for use, was practically new.

"Take out two," Nonna said, rolling to her side and lifting

the back of her shirt. You were supposed to peel the adhesive from the patch and stick it directly on the skin. I frowned, reading the box.

"Nonna, it says one at a time."

"That's okay, honey, I can do two," she said.

I hesitated. Unwelcome visions of Officer Hotchkiss shimmered before my eyes. "Abusing prescription drugs, Miss McCarthy?" the vision sneered.

"I don't know," I said reluctantly. "I think two is too much."

"Brett!" she said sharply. The tone surprised me. Panicky. A little angry. Nonna never spoke to me that way. "I need to sleep, and one patch just isn't going to do it."

I remember being glad that Nonna's face was turned away from me, her shoulder bones protruding like wings, as I gently pressed the patches to her back. Tears slid down my cheeks as I wondered whether I was poisoning my grandmother or helping her.

Nonna finally settled down. Her eyes closed, and she became very still. I thought she was asleep and, after replacing the box of patches in the medicine cabinet, crawled into my sleeping bag on the couch. I heard her say something.

"What, Nonna?" I asked.

"Like a poem," she murmured. "Like a poem, riding on its own melt." Then Nonna really was asleep, and I followed.

cru•el

"April is the cruelest month," my father always says in . . . guess . . . April. He doesn't just say it once. He says it all month, several times a day, no matter how many times you beg him to put a sock in it. But it's a quote from a famous poem, and since he's an English professor, that sort of stuff just pours out of him. Especially since we live in Maine, where April really stinks.

Cruel: *causing injury, grief, or pain; disposed to inflict suffering.*

In other places April is a terrific month, or so I've heard. People wear shorts and play ball. Cook burgers on the grill. In those other places it's called "spring," but here we call it "mud season." Daffodils may bloom in Jersey, but here grit-covered piles of dirty snow line the edges of driveways. They may be wearing Easter bonnets in Atlanta, but here little kids wrapped in parkas and mittens hunt for eggs.

I hate April almost as much as I hate poetry. Well . . . that might not be fair. I really don't hate poetry. You can't be a McCarthy and hate poetry. I just hate having it quoted at me all the time, especially when the weather is driving me bonkers.

Dad and I were spreading the last of the homemade strawberry jam on peanut butter sandwiches one rainy afternoon when he said it for, like, the fortieth time that week.

"This is the last jar of jam," I said, scraping the sides of the Ball jar with a knife. "No more until we pick strawberries in July. One more thing I hate about April: the end of last summer's jam."

"April is the cruelest month," Dad sighed.

I slammed the knife down in irritation. "Eliot is the cruelest poet," I snapped.

Dad looked at me with pleased surprise. "How did you know he wrote that?" Dad asked.

Whoops, I thought. "Don't get the wrong idea," I said.

"Have you been reading poetry when no one was looking?" Dad continued. "Dare I say it . . . reading *good* poetry?"

"Alls I did was look it up, okay?" I said, purposely inserting the grammatically incorrect "alls." It drives Dad up the wall when I use bad grammar. "I mean, if you're going to keep saying it, I wanted to at least know where it came from."

"And?" he said. I turned to face him.

"Dad. This 'April is the cruelest month' thing? It's not a poem. I mean, it practically has *chapters*. It has languages I've never heard of. It makes no sense. I think it's cruel you make your students read it."

Dad laughed. "Bravo!" he exclaimed. "Could it be that

you *are* my daughter, after all? And to think I've been worried for years that you were switched at birth with the child of professional athletes! But you have the McCarthy poetry gene after all!" He neatly sliced his sandwich in two, chuckling at his own joke.

I scowled at him. "Poetry obsession, more like," I groused.

We carried our plates to the kitchen island, munching in silence, watching through the bay windows as cold rain spattered the deck. Mom had just gone across the backyard to bring lunch to Nonna. She'd worn her Gore-Tex rain jacket and a fleece, sloshing through the grassy puddles and carrying a pot of soup. The house had been dark when she'd set out, but Dad and I could see lights burning now in the Gnome Home kitchen.

"You inherited it from Nonna," I said matter-of-factly. "This poetry thing."

"Actually, my father," he said. "That's one of the few things I remember about him. He was always reading, and it was usually poetry. Mother likes it, but it wasn't a passion for her the way it was for him."

"She and Mr. Beady argue about poems," I said.

"They argue about everything," Dad said ruefully.

"But she quotes poems, like you," I said. "You know that night I stayed with her? She was saying poems in her sleep."

"Really?" Dad said. "Can you remember what she said?"

"I only heard a few words," I said. "Something about

poems melting. Or was it poems riding? But it was poetry, I could tell."

"A poem rides on its own melt," Dad said quietly.

"That's it!" I said, surprised. "How did you know?"

"It's Frost," he said. "Robert Frost. And it's not a poem, but how he described how you write one. It's a very famous line, actually. For students of Frost. I'll be darned, Mother." He said this to himself, not me. I saw him stare through the cruel rain to the little house across the yard. The lights burned upstairs too, which should have been a signal to us. Nonna no longer slept upstairs but in a hospital bed on the first floor.

"You say she said this in her sleep?" he asked.

"Well . . . maybe right before she fell asleep," I said carefully. Hallucinated to sleep, I thought. Drugged to sleep, by her own granddaughter. I had never confessed to my parents about that night. When I woke that morning, Nonna was still out. So out that I was able to gently push her to one side and peel off a patch. I wrapped it in paper towels and buried it at the bottom of the kitchen trash can.

Nonna and I never spoke of it. I wasn't sure she even remembered.

"Well." Dad smiled at me. "She may be more of a poetry lover than I realized." Then the phone rang. It was Mom.

As he listened into the receiver, the calm look on my father's face morphed from concern to confusion to panic. He and Mom were rapid-firing questions and answers.

"Did you call the home health nurse?" he asked. Pause. "Well, *when* did she leave? What's the exact time?" Pause. "Did you call Beady?" Pause. "Are you sure you dialed the right number? He always leaves his answering machine on." Pause. "Did you look— No, never mind. I'm coming over." Dad hung up.

"Stay here," he said shortly.

"What's wrong?" I said, a sick, cold feeling spreading through my stomach.

"She's not there," Dad said. "At least your mom can't find her. Stay right here, Brett. In case the phone rings." He darted out the door, into the rain, without stopping for a jacket. I watched water splash with each footstep as he raced across the lawn.

Later I learned that he'd ordered me to stay because he didn't want me there if his hunch about Nonna were true. That she'd fallen. That despite her inability to dress herself without help or get out of the high hospital bed without an arm to lean on, she'd somehow walked across the room and fallen.

As it turns out, he was wrong. Nonna wasn't anywhere in or near the Gnome Home. She was simply gone. So were her hikers, her Michelin Man parka, and her raincoat. So were her island cap, her umbrella, and her fat-tired wheelchair. So were her pain patches. It didn't take a genius to figure out that Nonna wasn't simply missing. She had left.

And it didn't take a genius to guess who had packed up her

stuff and wheeled her away. Mr. Beady and Nonna were up to something.

I remember just feeling numb, while my parents clicked into search mode. Because I knew something that they didn't.

I had never spoken a word to anyone about the Nalgene bottle. Partially because Nonna had wanted to keep it to herself. Partially because it was too hard for me to think about what it meant. I sat in the kitchen while my parents dashed madly about, and it occurred to me that Nonna might have decided to go out and make things happen instead of waiting for things to happen. Maybe she'd decided to leave, spare us all—including herself—the full definition of "bad."

And I thought, Of course. This would happen in April. The cruelest month.

e·mote

"Where do you think they went?" I asked him.

Michael sighed at the other end of the phone. He had just gotten an earful: a complete download of everything from Nonna and Mr. Beady's Great Escape to the Nalgene and my thoughts about how cruel April can be. Serious emoting.

Emote: *to give expression to emotion.* Talk without interruption about something upsetting.

"Brett, first calm down. Take a deep breath. Things are never as bad as we imagine."

"Michael, I'm imagining that my grandmother has left us and is trying to off herself. It's pretty bad."

"Brett, please." He paused. When he spoke again, it was from *The Lord of the Rings: The Two Towers.* We've watched it together about three dozen times.

"What does your heart tell you?" I heard Aragorn say.

"I don't know!" I wailed. I really didn't. My heart pounded

too loudly for me to hear anything but jungle drumming. I took a deep breath and tried. Something whispered.

"Frodo is alive," I replied. I did a lousy Gandalf, but Michael got it.

"Good," he said, back to Michael. "Now let's use our heads."

"Mine hurts," I replied.

"Where have your parents already looked?"

"They've called the hospital and the hospice place. They've called a bunch of her friends. They've driven to the movie theater, the coffee shop, and the library. Michael, she's disappeared."

"No one just disappears," he said. "Think. Where would she *like* to go? You have to figure Mr. Beady didn't take her someplace awful. Any chance they went to the airport?"

"Dad's on his way to Portland now. He tried telephoning the Jetport with her description, but they weren't very helpful, so he's going in person. I think he'll end up cruising the parking lot looking for Mr. Beady's pickup."

Silence from the other end, as we thought. I stared out the kitchen window. The rain had finally let up, and it had gotten windy. Cold, windy, and raw. A great day to travel with an old, sick woman, I thought. What could be worse?

A totally wild thought crossed my mind. Something extraordinarily worse.

"Can you hang on for one minute?" I said, dropping the

phone before Michael had a chance to answer. I ran to the mudroom, slipped into some boots, and darted outside in the direction of the Gnome Home garage.

The late-afternoon light filtered dully through the dusty windows. I knew exactly what to look for: a round wooden pallet covered in oilcloth. I switched on the overhead bulb. Light filled the room. Filled the empty space that told me exactly what I needed to know. I dashed back to the house.

"The light's gone," I panted into the receiver. No comment. "Michael! Are you there?"

"The light?" he said.

"Your project! The lanterns, the reflectors, the big round board you put them on! They've been in the garage all winter, and now they're gone."

"Geez, talk about a bad day," he groaned. "First your grandmother takes off, now you get robbed!"

"Hello? I thought *you* were the smart one! Don't you see? Nobody's robbed anything. They took the lights *with* them."

It was nuts. But why else would they have kept it so secret? Never in a zillion years would my parents have approved of this one. Garage sales, bazooka birthdays, lighthouse projects . . . all wacky but still within the safe part of the sanity meter. But a trip to the island this time of year?

"Whoa," Michael said. "Not good."

"It makes sense, doesn't it?"

"Call your parents. Now," he said. Urgency in his voice. His line clicked off.

I reached Dad on his cell phone. He'd driven as far as Yarmouth, about twenty minutes from the Jetport.

"I don't think so, hon," he replied when I finished spilling our theory. "To begin with, I know where the lights went. Beady moved them to Dwayne's. Along with some lumber." Dwayne Morin was a friend of Mr. Beady's. He owned the boatyard where we docked the *Dolly* and where we always departed for Spruce Island.

"That just proves what I've said!" I exclaimed. "See? He can just stick everything in a boat and motor over."

"I've talked to Beady about this," Dad said, a little impatiently. "You may not believe it, but there's a plan. A rational, reasonable plan that does not involve dangerous off-season trips. Now Brett, your grandmother is a smart woman. She wouldn't do something foolish."

"Daddy, please," I continued. "There's something you don't know. I think . . . I think Nonna is afraid of losing us. And I think . . . she doesn't want to die. So . . ."

"So she's decided to basically kill herself by boating out to the island in the freezing cold?" he exclaimed angrily. "Don't be ridiculous, Brett. Let me tell you something: You're not the only one who loves her. Or knows her. She's been my mother for many more years than she's been your grandmother, and I think I know a little bit more about her. So please . . . let's hang up the phone and keep the line clear in case we get any *real* news." His phone went dead.

In my dictionary the definition of "alone" has no words. It

has a picture. A picture of a girl, in a dark kitchen, stupidly holding a silent telephone receiver. She stares out the windows at a vacant, lifeless house across the lawn. And there is no sound except this rhythmic throbbing in her chest.

I pressed speed dial, then 1.

"Michael," I said, then stopped, because I couldn't choke out the rest.

"I'm on my way," he said.

diss

At the deep, dark heart of every junior high kid's soul lies fear of The Diss.

Webster's Collegiate Dictionary defines it as both a verb . . . *to treat with disrespect; insult, criticize* (as in "She's dissed!") . . . and a noun (as in "What a diss!"). Depending on who does the dissing, it might be funny or mean: a lighthearted comment tossed between friends or a wooden stake to the heart. It might hurt like a burn and scar forever, or it might simply evaporate, forgotten, with a smile.

Dad's diss felt like the burning, wooden-stake variety. Which explains what followed.

Ten minutes after Michael hung up, I saw the lights of Aunt Lorena's car pull into our driveway. I started for the door, but Michael burst into the kitchen without knocking. "What did your dad say?" he asked immediately.

I shook my head miserably.

"He doesn't want to hear it," I said. "Anything I say just pisses him off."

He settled heavily into a kitchen chair, his rain slicker dripping on the tile floor.

"Same here," he said in a grumpy voice. "Although my folks weren't pissed. They just gave me the absentminded-professor treatment. Patted me on the head and suggested I find some nice Russian to play chess with online." He kicked the leg of the chair, hard. "I'm their kid who understands the theory of relativity but can't remember my shorts for gym class, you know?"

"Well, at least they brought you over," I said. "Did you tell them I was freaking out?"

"They didn't bring me over," he said.

"Huh? I saw your car pull up."

Michael looked at me intently. "I brought myself over," he said carefully. His eyes locked on mine.

"Tell me this is *not* what I think it is," I said nervously.

Michael reached into his pocket and pulled out a set of car keys. He swung them, teasingly, before his grinning face.

"Are you out of your mind?" I gasped. "You drive . . . in a car . . . by yourself? You could get killed, or arrested. Or kill somebody else! Jeezum, Michael!"

"I once went as far as Portland and back," he replied

calmly. I stared at him. This was a side of Michael I'd never dreamed existed.

"Promise me you'll stop," I said, dead serious. "No joke. You could get in big, bad trouble. Trust me, I know trouble."

I wondered, for one hopeful moment, if he was having a good laugh at me. If Aunt Lorena was outside, hiding in the car, and this was all just a ploy to help me lighten up.

No such luck.

"I think we should go to Morin's Landing," he said. "There's this totally awesome boat there, and I know where the owners keep a key. You know where she is, Brett. We both know it."

Morin's Landing. Where our family docked the *Dolly Llama* and always set off for Spruce Island. I closed my eyes and shook my head. I didn't want to consider this, any of it. Not Nonna missing, not Michael driving, not Brett stealing boats and taking off on crazy schemes. I wanted, for like the zillionth time, to turn back the clock, to get back to normal. In other words, the way things were before redefinition.

But an imaginary voice whispered in my ear: ain't gonna happen, kid. Your grandmother isn't going to magically appear at the door, cancer-free and carrying a pan of hot brownies. Your father isn't going to believe a thing you say. Your former friends aren't going to help you because they've moved on, to hot guys and pom-poms. And your new friends are home studying calculus.

"Are you sure you know what you're doing?" I asked for the first time.

It wouldn't be the last.

pre·car·i·ous

Here's the thing about driving in Maine: Kids do it.

Especially in the rural areas and unorganized territories. In The County, kids helping with the potato harvest learn to handle tractors. Fishermen's kids and island kids drive power-boats. In the North Woods, where you can't get groceries in the winter unless you can operate a snowmobile, I'll bet more than half the kids can drive them.

Of course, cars are a completely different story. I'd never heard of an eighth grader cruising in an automobile on the highway. Or being nuts enough to try.

Nevertheless, Sockrgurl found herself safety-belted into the passenger seat of a Subaru wagon in the wee hours of an April night, as MensaMan drove her along Route One. I kept looking in the side-view mirror for flashing blue police lights. I kept checking the speedometer, making sure he didn't exceed the limit. I kept pinching myself, hoping this was a bad dream.

"What's our story if you get pulled over?" I asked.

"We're not going to get pulled over," he replied patiently.

"Maybe you can tell them you're temporarily insane," I suggested. "Or permanently. You can act really surprised when they accuse you of being an underage driver."

"It won't matter, because I don't have a license," he said. "The penalties for operating without a license are identical for the sane or the insane. I've checked."

"I wonder if they'll make you take a Breathalyzer," I continued. "I mean, they'll figure you've got to be drunk. Or worse."

"Or maybe it's all three, you know?" he said. "I'm mentally deranged, drunk, and drugged. And if they ask me my name, I'll tell them it's . . . Hotchkiss! Michael Hotchkiss. And that my dad taught me everything I know about drugs and alcohol." We both laughed.

"You know, speaking of our favorite teacher . . . there's something I've been wondering about," I said. "How did you know all that stuff about marijuana?"

Michael shrugged. "It's no secret. It's on the Internet."

"Yeah, but why were you even reading about it?"

"Just Googling one day. I don't really remember."

"You Googled 'pot'?"

"No, I Googled 'cancer,' " he said.

I was quiet for a while, thinking.

"That surprises you?" he asked.

I shrugged. "No. It's just that sometimes I forget I'm not the only one who cares."

"I think sometimes you forget that not everyone in the world is a lousy friend."

"That too," I agreed. "Remind me, if you don't wrap us around a tree tonight, to thank you for being an incredible friend."

"I'm involved now," he said in a familiar yet non-Michael voice. "You let go and I'm going to have to jump in there after you."

"Oh, don't tell me, don't tell me . . . yes! I know! Leonardo DiCaprio as Jack Dawson, in *Titanic*!" I exclaimed triumphantly.

"Very good," he said, sounding surprised.

"I have to ask you something else," I said. "Truth?" He nodded.

"Is Nonna smoking pot?"

Michael sighed.

"The truth?" he asked. "I have no clue. I told her and Mr. Beady about the medical marijuana stuff. Your grandmother thought it was funny, like wouldn't it be a riot if she became an old-lady pothead. But Mr. Beady asked for the Web sites. I don't know if he ever did anything about it. Has it gotten that bad?"

"Yeah, it has," I answered softly, gazing out the window. We'd exited Route One and now snaked along the windy roads that led to the ocean. Inky black outside. No street-lights, not a sign of life from all the dark houses. Then I saw something flash in the side-view mirror. Distant, moving in the same direction as us.

"Headlights," I said, my heart sinking. Since turning onto

the rural road, we'd traveled alone. We were close to the Landing, and I'd begun to think we were actually going to make it.

"Drive steady," I said. "It's probably someone who lives out here, going home."

"Or not," he said. "I'm pulling over."

"That'll just attract attention!" I exclaimed. "They'll think you broke down."

"Brett, it's almost two in the morning, and people around here are all sleeping because they have to get up in a couple of hours to take their fishing boats out. Chances are that's a cop. Even if he's not looking for *us*, he's looking." Just then a wide dirt parking lot opened to our left. It surrounded a clapboard, barnlike building bearing a large sign, JOHNSON MARINE, BUILDING AND REPAIRS. Without hitting the turn signal and without slowing down, Michael swerved into the lot and cut the lights. For a moment, before our eyes adjusted to the darkness, it was like floating through space. We could see nothing but felt ourselves propelled forward in the moving car.

"Michael!" I screamed. It was terrifying, flying blind like this. I braced myself for the impact. Michael switched on the parking lights, and two small beams illuminated the space a few feet in front of the car. It was enough to allow him to guide us alongside the building, right up to the edge of the woods bordering the lot. When we stopped, he cut the engine and turned off the lights again.

Way in the distance bright headlights flickered as they

passed behind trees and drew closer. They weren't going particularly fast, but they were definitely headed in our direction, along the marina road. Neither of us spoke; just waited.

Within a few minutes a pickup drove past, its radio playing so loudly I could feel the bass throb right through the floorboards of our car. It sped by without pause, into the night, eventually no more than two red taillights in the distance. We both sighed.

"The fishermen are awake now," I commented.

"Right," said Michael. "Let's get out of here before the cops who might be chasing *them* find us instead."

Morin's Landing is a small family-owned marina run by part-time lobsterman, part-time outboard motor mechanic, Dwayne Morin. He's old, like Mr. Beady and Nonna, and unlike Mr. Beady, he's a real Mainer. Whenever we load bags into the *Dolly Llama*, or carry heavy coolers packed with ice down the long dock, and he says, "Let me help you with that, *deah*," it's the real thing. We'd docked our boat at the landing for as long as I could remember. Still, it looked completely different in the dark.

Hulking shadows of sailboats yet to be put in for the season crowded one end of the parking lot like beached whales. Over the front door of the small frame building Mr. Morin used as a workshop and office, a blue neon security light buzzed. Steel lobster traps, stacked seven to eight high, stood sentry near the ramp leading to the water. At low tide that ramp sloped steeply downward, a precarious descent.

Precarious: *dependent on chance circumstances, unknown conditions, or uncertain developments.* Dangerous.

As Michael steered the car into a parking space alongside the traps, I could see the ramp, floating almost horizontal to the land. High tide. That helped. Took us down a few notches on the Precarious Meter.

I grabbed flashlights and raincoats from the backseat. Michael reached into the glove compartment, pulling out a plastic rectangular box about the size of an iPod.

"Tunes?" I said. "Are you kidding?"

"Global positioning system. Handheld with navigation capabilities. No genius travels without one," he said matter-of-factly.

"I really hope you know what you're doing," I breathed as we stepped out. An icy, wet wind gusted into my face.

I waited for Michael on the ramp while he went to fetch the key to the power dory we planned to "borrow." About a half dozen boats, tied to iron rings along the dock, bobbed in the water. I swept the line of them with my flashlight. At the end of the line I saw the *Dolly Llama*. My heart sank.

They weren't here. Mr. Beady didn't own a boat, and despite his long list of annoying qualities, stealing boats wasn't among them. If the *Dolly* was here, then Nonna wasn't.

I saw Michael dart across the lot.

"Got it!" he panted, holding up a key attached to a silver chain.

"How did you know where it was?" I marveled.

"I'm Superman, Lois," he said. Christopher Reeve, from the movie *Superman*.

"Michael, seriously. You didn't bust into the office—"

"Chill," he said, laughing quietly. "The owner parks his boat trailer here and leaves the spare key on top of one of the tires. C'mon, let's go." He nudged me toward the ramp.

"They're not here," I said dully. "Look." I aimed my flashlight at the *Dolly*.

But Michael just shrugged.

"They wouldn't have taken the *Dolly*," he said. "She doesn't handle well in this sort of weather. Not like this baby!"

Michael directed the beam of his flashlight toward a long white boat tied to the dock. Even in the dark I could tell she was new.

"It's a pretty big dory," I said skeptically. "Are you sure you can—"

"Trust me, Rose. Do you trust me?" He was back to *Titanic* dialogue, Leonardo DiCaprio playing Jack Dawson.

Trust him? I wasn't even sure I trusted myself.

dis•as•ter

I hadn't counted on the cold.

Scary cold. Forget bone-chilling; this was marrow-freezing. The ocean off the coast of Maine is part of the same North Atlantic where the *Titanic* sank. Minus the icebergs, but just as dead cold as that April when the big ship went down.

Michael managed to point this out as the salty black chop of the water sprayed against the sides of the power dory and into our faces. The boat wasn't going fast, but the wind kept stirring things up.

"It hurts," I said, willing my teeth not to chatter. "The water actually hurts."

"Water that cold?" said Michael in his Jack Dawson imitation. "It hits you like a thousand knives, stabbing you all over your body. You can't breathe, you can't think . . . at least not about anything but the pain."

I groaned. At that moment I failed to see the humor in replaying scenes from *Titanic*.

"Actually, a body can survive only fifteen minutes in water this cold," said Michael, back to his Michael voice. "I looked it up."

Great, I thought. I'm going to freeze to death at two a.m. in a stolen boat driven by the captain of the Mescataqua Junior High School Math Team. I imagined the headlines: "Suspended Soccer Star and School Brainiac Perish in Icy Boating Accident." The papers would carry photos of the wrecked dory. Interviews with our puzzled friends. The pissed-off dory owner. They would wonder: What were those kids doing out there? Good question.

"Brett! Hold the flashlight steady!" Michael said, a little sharply, pulling me from my morbid thoughts. I directed the beam onto the floor of the boat, where he'd placed the GPS. Last summer, with my dad, he'd programmed the starting location (Morin's) and destination (Spruce Island) into the GPS. Now, as long as we followed the directions it gave, we could navigate in the dark, past the rocks and right up to the island's dock. Miles overhead the eyes of some giant satellite bore down on us, tracking our movements.

"Are you sure you know what you're doing?" I repeated.

"Trust me, Rose. Do you trust me?" he replied, back to *Titanic* dialogue.

"If you don't stop imitating Leonardo, I'm going to push you overboard," I said. "And you'll have only fifteen minutes left in your incredibly annoying life."

We rode in silence after that, listening to the monotonous,

low drone of the engine. The smaller islands glided past, darker shadows against the dark sky. The moon hid behind filmy clouds that covered the stars as well. It was a bitter, unfriendly night, and it made me sad. Sadder than I had been even in the past months, and I felt suddenly overwhelmed by the stupidity of it all.

This was a mistake. Once again I had let my emotions rule my common sense. But unlike all the previous disasters, the consequences here could be deadly. This water was freakin' cold, and we couldn't see a thing.

Disaster: *a calamitous event bringing great damage, loss, or destruction.*

I had opened my mouth to tell Michael to turn the boat around and take us back to shore when we saw it. The glow.

From a modern lighthouse the beam knocks you flat. The twenty-first-century fog-piercing ray penetrates gray ocean mist like a laser. People who value their eyesight avoid looking straight into it at close range. This glow, however, was something else entirely. Instead of laser white, it burned gold. Instead of a sharp arrow, it was a soft halo. From the top of Spruce Island lighthouse, which had been dark for a hundred years, it welcomed us now.

"It works. It works!" Michael exclaimed, raising his fist in the air. "Yes!"

My eyes filled with tears. I was too exhausted and cold to pump the air like Michael, but that glow was my victory too. I was right. She was here. And I had been so close to turning back.

As we approached the Spruce Island dock, Michael cut the engine way back and steered the dory carefully alongside. I jumped out, rope in hand, and tied us up. Michael jumped out behind me.

"Okay, let's go," he breathed into my ear. We took off at a run, our flashlights strafing the path with beams that bounced at every step.

Ages ago, way before Nonna and my grandfather bought the island, or were even born, for that matter, Spruce Island had been a farm. Not much of a farm. "Subsistence farm," according to my father, which meant a family lived there, probably fished, and ate what they planted. There are open meadowy spaces in the middle with bent fruit trees that still produce an occasional apple or pear. Little footpaths crisscross the entire island, from a small sandy beach through the balsam "fairy woods" to the old lighthouse on the point. Michael and I followed the path to the middle of the island.

"Let's start with the cottages," I panted.

"Why not the lighthouse?" he said.

"Because I smell smoke," I replied. "Someone's lit a fire."

No light shone when we entered the clearing. The deserted look of the place creeped me out. The four cottages, arranged in a semicircle with a big open space in the front for bonfires, gaped at us with dark, blind eyes. The pine trees thrashed overhead in the wind, and the bonfire place was dead cold.

"Do you think they're inside one of the little houses, sleeping?" Michael whispered.

"Nonna! Mr. Beady!" I yelled. "Where are you guys?"

Nothing. I aimed my flashlight at the rooftops. From one protruded a metal cylinder, thin tendrils of gray smoke oozing from its top. Michael and I looked at each other, nodded, and dashed toward it.

The door swung inward at our push. Right off I noticed two things. First, the heat. The inside of the cottage was way warmer than the outdoors. In the little sitting room to our left I could hear dry wood pop and see orange glowing behind the grill of a small iron stove. The second thing: clutter. I saw a duffel bag, open, with half its contents strewn on the floor; a big cooler, cover half off, filled with groceries.

No question about it: Mr. Beady had been here.

Michael had tiptoed ahead of me into the bedroom. He emerged, shaking his head.

"Empty," he said. "But it looks like someone's been lying in the bed. Covers are all rumpled."

"Let's try the lighthouse," I said, exasperated.

The path from the cottages to the lighthouse is the deepest, most heavily wooded on Spruce Island. On the hottest and brightest of summer days this path remains cold and shadowy. Year round it smells like Christmas trees in there, and tiny mammals, like red squirrels and chipmunks, rule. It's the sort of place Monique Rose would love, and where I'd already promised to build fairy houses with her come summer.

But on a raw April night at three a.m. it's one scary place. We had to walk slowly, since the combination of ankle-turning roots and pitch dark didn't lend itself to running. The trees, swaying in the wind, moaned. I don't know what made me do it, but I reached out and grabbed Michael's hand.

It was amazingly warm. I remember feeling incredibly grateful to have that hand to hang on to, and as we made our way through the woods, I gripped it with bone-crushing intensity. Michael never complained—which is saying something, because I have pretty powerful paws. As we approached the end of the path, the sound of waves washing up on the rocks grew louder.

And suddenly we were there. The woods opened, and Spruce Island lighthouse blazed before us. Well, maybe "blazed" isn't exactly accurate. Compared to the dark path and view of the lighthouse from the water, it seemed blazing, close up. It was definitely bright, and on a clear night could probably have been seen for miles. The lanterns, glowing from atop the stone tower, flickered when the wind gusted hard against the windows. They illuminated the air, heavy with moisture, so everything around us seemed bathed in gold.

Michael released my hand, taking a few steps to his right in order to get a better look. He crashed into something and swore.

"What the . . . ," he said, then gasped. In the dim light I

could make out two shapes. Not standing, not lying on the ground, but seated. Reclining, actually. In aluminum beach chairs. They did not look human. The only thing I can compare them to is larvae. That disgusting, maggot-like stage of insect development: white, cocoon-like, and bloated. Only these larvae were giant, man-sized mutants.

"Oh my god!" Michael screamed, his voice high-pitched with fear. "Mummies!"

sol·i·tar·y

Larvae, mummies, whatever. Equally horrible, especially when the biggest of the two larvae-mummies reared its head at Michael's scream. It pulled itself into an upright sitting position, like a big L.

"Michael? Brett? What are you doing here?" it said in Mr. Beady's voice.

Of course: mummy sleeping bags. Nonna used them whenever Elders United for Peace and Social Justice held their annual winter solstice party. They'd all zip themselves snugly into the bags, settle into reclining chairs on the Gnome Home lawn, and peacefully contemplate the stars overhead in the cold night sky. The bags fit over their heads and tied securely at their chins, leaving just a small round opening at the face for breathing. Comfy and warm, the elders didn't care one bit that the bags made them resemble giant insect larvae.

They made perfect sense on a cruel April night, in wind and fog.

I knelt beside the smaller mummy.

"Nonna?"

There was her face, poking from the head of the sleeping bag. Her eyelids flickered. She'd been asleep.

"Hi, hon," she said dreamily. I wasn't sure she knew me.

"Nonna, it's Brett. Are you okay?" She smiled, and her gaze wandered from my face to something directly over my head.

"Look," she said softly.

I twisted around. From where she reclined, Nonna had a great view. The lighthouse loomed overhead, a golden beacon that outshone everything. We couldn't see the mortar crumbling off the tower, or the peeling paint, the rusty steel bars of the catwalk, the cracked windows. Only the perfect, lovely light. It was surreal, as if the combination of darkness, fog, and flame had taken us back in time, to the first night some solitary keeper climbed this tower and lit the lanterns.

Solitary: *alone*.

"Isn't it amazing?" Nonna said quietly. "Such little things. Candles, really. Look how much light just a little candle makes!"

I didn't bother to argue with her. Didn't bother to point out that these were actually sixteen lanterns, with reflectors, and not one little candle. She seemed so pleased and peaceful, and it seemed ages since she'd rested. I wondered how many fentanyl patches it had taken to get her to this state. I sat on the wet gravel, my blue-jeaned bottom immediately soaked, and rested my head on her shoulder.

The four of us stayed like that for a long time. Michael and Mr. Beady spoke quietly to each other, Michael grilling him on every detail related to transporting and erecting the lanterns. Nonna drifted in and out of sleep, occasionally murmuring something I couldn't understand. I hunched down into my raincoat, cheek on the cold, damp mummy bag, and tried to relax myself warm.

It occurred to me that this moment, this strange little scene on the beach, had been my reason all along for coming. Deep down I had known Nonna would never do anything to harm herself or hurt our feelings. Deeper down . . . pretty deep, actually . . . I knew Mr. Beady would take care of her, and certainly didn't need me and Michael to come to the rescue. I had simply wanted to be with her when she saw her lighthouse blaze.

Because there wasn't going to be a Memorial Day trip to the island for Nonna. We were that close to the end. The Former Queen of Denial understood that. I understood, the way I understand sunrises, tide changes, and orbiting planets. I don't really *get* how they work, but I accept their existence. I have no choice.

I didn't realize it then, but the redefinition that had

kicked off on October 16th was almost complete. Since that afternoon, sometime after four p.m., I had shed and added more defining characteristics than I even knew existed. I had just one more to lose, and it would happen in a few days: "Only Granddaughter."

hy·po·ther·mic

My body was sending all sorts of hypothermic distress signals. Uncontrollable shaking, for example. I kept thinking of the woodstove back at the cottage. I also figured that if I was this cold, Nonna might be as well.

Hypothermic: *having a subnormal body temperature.*

"Mr. Beady!" I hissed. Two heads turned toward me. "What time is it?" The big larva twisted, and I heard unzipping sounds.

"Four," he said.

"Don't you think we should get her inside?" I said.

Mr. Beady shrugged off his mummy bag and emerged fully clothed, even down to his heavy winter boots. He bent over Nonna, whose soft, even breathing made little puffs of steam, and lifted her in his arms. For an old guy, Mr. Beady is one tough bird. Even though Nonna was a featherweight, any sleeping person feels like a dead weight.

Michael and I grabbed the chairs and followed him down

the dark fairy path to the cottages. He walked carefully, but then I saw him stumble over a root.

"Nonna!" I exclaimed. Mr. Beady regained his footing and kept moving ahead.

It's amazing what a little adrenaline can do. It gives you the zooms, the energy to do what needs to be done. That moment, when I thought Mr. Beady was going to hit the ground and land on Nonna, adrenaline shot through me like an arrow, and I forgot all about my shivering legs, shaking like jelly.

"Let us take her; you're tired," I insisted.

"No, no," Mr. Beady muttered, plodding ahead. "I've got her."

"No you don't," I said, standing directly in front of him and dropping my chair. "You're exhausted." I reached both arms under Nonna's shoulders and lifted so her head rested on my chest. Michael dropped his chair and did the same with her legs, and we gently hefted her from Mr. Beady's arms. Together we continued along the dark path.

I don't think I've ever been so happy to see anything as that white-shingled cottage. The muscles in my arms burned, my breath came short and fast, and in the space of a few hundred yards I'd gone from totally cold to sweating. Mr. Beady opened the door ahead of us, so Michael and I walked inside, straight to the bedroom, and laid Nonna on the bed. I unzipped the wet mummy bag and pulled and tugged until I'd extricated her from it.

Mr. Beady had her all duded out in the Michelin Man parka and every other warm thing she owned. I ran my hands over her: dry as a nut. What's more, she never woke up. Slept right through it all, which was a miracle since she hadn't been comfortable in weeks. I sat alongside her, listening to her quiet, even breathing.

When I returned to the sitting room, Michael was stuffing split logs into the woodstove. Mr. Beady was banging around in the kitchen. Each cottage has a small propane stove, and he was setting a kettle of water to boil for tea. I collapsed into an armchair, too shattered to remove my wet raincoat, and stared at the orange coals flickering to life under Michael's hands.

Mr. Beady rejoined us in the sitting room, pulling a chair alongside mine.

"Where are your parents?" he asked us. Michael and I looked at each other and shrugged. Mr. Beady narrowed his eyes suspiciously.

"How did you get out here?" he continued.

"Same as you," Michael replied. "Drove to the Landing. Took a boat over."

"By yourselves?" Mr. Beady asked. We nodded. He stared at us for a moment, uncomprehending. When he understood that we'd come out alone, he groaned softly and put his head in his hands.

"They're going to kill me," he said. "They're going to think I put you up to this."

"Actually, they're going to kill you for dragging Nonna out

here," I commented. "With all due respect, Mr. Beady . . . what were you thinking?"

"I took every precaution!" he cried. "She was never in any danger. Dwayne and I made sure of that."

"Dwayne Morin?" Michael asked.

"He brought us over in his fishing boat," Mr. Beady explained. "Much bigger than the *Dolly Llama*. And got her up to the cottages using the lawn mower. You know, the big driving mower? Dwayne attached a trailer to it. We propped Eileen between the duffels in the trailer, with the cooler, and drove her right up the path." I imagined the look of horror on my mother's face when she heard all this.

"The lanterns?" Michael continued.

"I set them up a day earlier," Mr. Beady said. "I've had them in Morin's workshop for weeks now."

"You've been planning this for weeks?" I exclaimed. Mr. Beady shook his head and stared into the fire. The wood burned bright now, and the room felt warm.

"I was thinking of the summer," he said quietly. "This trip just . . . happened." He looked at me, his eyes wide with a question. Asking me if I understood why he'd done this.

Absolutely.

The three of us remained quiet in the dark room, Michael occasionally feeding logs to the flames. At some point the kettle screamed, and Mr. Beady got up to make tea. Sometime in there I slipped off my raincoat and hung it on a peg. Dripping water formed a circle beneath it. I wrapped my hands around the hot mug Mr. Beady handed me, amazed at the intense pleasure of clutching something warm. Nonna coughed.

"Beady?" she said quietly. We both jumped up.

She was a slight bump beneath a mound of blankets we'd heaped on her. Mr. Beady sat gently on the edge of the bed and looked intently into her face. In the dim light I saw her smile at him.

"Eileen, how are you feeling?"

"Peachy," she replied. "Except these blankets smell like mothballs."

"I'll take that up with the management, next time I see them," he replied. He winked at me. "Could you do with some tea?" She nodded, and looked beyond him to where I stood. With difficulty, she pulled one arm from beneath the blankets and extended her hand.

Old people have these dry, thin hands. It makes me think of bird bones wrapped in Japanese rice paper. Only Nonna's were cold.

"Are you okay?" I asked her. "I heard they brought you in on a trailer."

"That didn't go so well," she admitted. "But I'm good now. I'm glad you're here, honey."

"Me too, Nonna."

"It's just like we imagined," she said. "When we bought the island, years ago? We dreamed of making it work again. Do you think it's silly? Do you think I'm foolish, dragging poor Beady out here?"

265

"I think he did the dragging," I said. "And no. I don't think it's silly. I think it's amazing." She closed her eyes, and her head sank a bit deeper into the pillows. Like she was melting. Just talking exhausted her.

We heard it then: the outboard motor. Sound travels easily over water, with nothing to get in its way. So there was no telling how far the boat was from the island. But the sound was getting louder, which meant closer. Mr. Beady appeared in the doorway, holding a mug.

"That's odd," he said, frowning. "Dwayne isn't due here for hours."

"I wonder if they see the light," she said. "Did you leave the lanterns burning?"

Mr. Beady looked at me.

"Of course," he said. Nonna smiled.

"Lovely," she said. "I like to think they see our light."

It was still dark outside. I imagined the bright halogen lights of—what? a police boat? a posse of angry fishermen recovering the stolen dory?—plowing through the cold, choppy water, pulling up to the Spruce Island dock.

Lovely? Scary, more like.

in·de·fin·a·ble

Two days later she was gone.

It's impossible to explain how I felt. Some feelings have no words. They're just . . . indefinable.

Indefinable: *incapable of being precisely described or analyzed.*

Dad says that's the whole point of the "April is the cruelest month" poem. He says in the end words fail. In the end we can only hope for peace so deep that it's beyond what our puny little minds can absorb. I get that, actually. So since I can find no way to define losing Nonna, I wait for the hollow place inside me to fill again. I go through the motions every day and trust that there will eventually come a morning when my first waking thought isn't "She's dead."

The outboard motor turned out to be Dwayne Morin's fishing boat. And my parents. And the rest of the Emergency Contact card. Aunt Lorena had discovered Michael missing, then the car missing, then called my parents, who told her about my idea. . . . You get the picture. Like a long line of dominoes, one knocks into the other, and next thing you know you've set off a chain reaction from Mescataqua to Spruce Island. We were all less than happy to see each other. Mom couldn't look Mr. Beady in the eye, she was that pissed. Dwayne Morin kept apologizing. Aunt Lorena and Uncle Jack kept thinking of more and more punishments for Michael: "No TV for a year! We're cutting off your allowance! Online chess is history!"

The only calm person was Nonna. When Dad, in all his panic, rushed into the bedroom to find her, she smiled dreamily at him.

"Did you see the light?" she asked softly, before she fell asleep again.

As soon as it got bright enough outside to see the roots and rocks along the path to the water, we hitched up the lawn mower trailer again. I got in first, sort of a human cushion for Nonna. We stuffed the duffels around us and bumped slowly back to the boat. She didn't say much but every once in a while gave a little groan. Mom walked alongside the trailer, and I could see her jaw tighten every time it lurched.

It took us all morning to get Nonna home. All day, actually. First carrying her carefully into Dwayne's boat, then out of the boat and up the ramp and into the car . . . For the life of me I don't know how Mr. Beady managed to get her to the island to begin with. It occurred to me he might be Superman or something, wearing full-body Lycra underwear under his flannel shirts, a big S emblazoned on the chest. I would have liked to tell Nonna that one. Mr. Beady in a Superman body suit.

But she never woke up.

From the moment we left the island until we finally got her back to her bed in the Gnome Home, Nonna grew quieter and quieter. Her breathing became shallow, coming out in soft, irregular whispers. She went from talking in her sleep to muttering things we couldn't understand to simply moving her lips soundlessly; speech abandoned her. She became very, very still. I watched her chest rise and fall, so slightly you could barely tell she moved. Sometimes a long while would pass between breaths, and I would think, "That's it." Then she'd give a little shudder and her lungs would fill again.

When she finally left us, it was morning, and we were all together. Light streamed into the living room, where we'd set up her hospital bed, and it smelled like the coffee Mom had just made. Mom sat in the rocker near the foot of the bed, while Mr. Beady had taken up residence in an armchair near the window. Dad and I sat on either side of Nonna. She took up so little space. He was holding her hand, watching her face, when her chest simply failed to rise. We waited. And finally he said, "She's gone." Then Dad bent his head, and his shoulders shook.

There are no words to describe the sound of your own father crying.

re·de·fined

I hadn't counted on the heat. Nasty heat. Humid, out-of-season, early heat that catches you unawares when your skin is still pasty winter white and you haven't gotten used to wearing shorts yet. The type of out-of-season heat wave that causes a run on fans at Rite Aid and gives overweight people heart palpitations.

Michael manages to bring up that delightful fact as the sweat pours off us one bright afternoon. We are clearing out the Gnome Home garage, by order of the Great Almighty Clearer Outer: Mom. The lease on the house is due to run out by the end of May, and we are busy removing every trace of Nonna, from the kitchen to the attic to the garage. None of us can bear throwing anything away, so what we don't *give* away we pack into our house or have Mr. Beady truck to his garage. He seems grateful to be busy. I wonder what he will do with himself once we finish the job.

"You know, people drop dead in this sort of weather," Michael pants. Perspiration forms two wet patches under the arms of his gray T-shirt and soaks the hair on the back of his neck. Helping the McCarthys Clear Out is Punishment #337 handed down by Uncle Jack and Aunt Lorena to their newly redefined son.

Michael Dwyer: *Online Chess Grand Master, Law-Abiding High Honors Student, Trustworthy Good Kid.*

Now:

Michael Dwyer, Redefined: *Underage Driver, Thief, Sneak, Brett McCarthy's Hero.*

"Thanks—now I'm really having fun," I remark. We dig through stacks of cardboard boxes. The contents are completely random. Some contain long-forgotten McCarthy family treasures, like Dad's junior high yearbooks from the 1970s. Others are filled with old bank statements, moldy shoes, yellowing envelopes . . . trash. You don't know what you might find, so you have to go through it all. Just in case.

Clearing out the house is way easier. That's because Nonna left a list. Short and sweet, which really helps. For example, she'd written: Florence, World's Fair Spoon Collection; Kathy Livingston, snowshoes and cross-country skis; Beady, my fly-fishing pole and tackle. It saves us having to think about who might like what, and for that last act of generosity my parents are extremely grateful. Thinking too much still brings their tears, but sorting, packing, sweeping, mailing . . . that they can handle.

Michael and I have sorted through maybe half the garage when the Great Almighty Clearer Outer decides to have mercy on us.

"You guys want some lemonade?" Mom stands at the entrance carrying a tray with a tall pitcher and two glasses. We don't need a second invitation. Filling the glasses, we wander over to the hammock in my yard. We ease ourselves, crossways, onto the ropes, swinging gently as we sip.

"So . . . are you coming this weekend?" I ask him.

Mom, Dad, and I, plus Mr. Beady, plus Mrs. Augmentino and the Fifth Period Class, are going to Spruce Island. This is the weekend we McCarthys traditionally open the cottage windows, beat dusty blankets with sticks, and sweep mouse poop from the floors. It is the weekend we usually move Nonna to the island, the *Dolly Llama* low in the water, weighed down by Nonna's bags. Instead, Mr. Beady is going to fire up the lighthouse, and I will build fairy houses with Monique Rose.

It is the first island weekend without Nonna, and I don't think I can bear it if Michael is missing too. But Punishment #85 is No Going Back to the Island This Year.

"It took a lot . . . and I mean *a lot* . . . of begging, but they agreed to let me come. I told them I didn't want to let you down, and that did it."

Michael's eyes are about six inches from mine, so he can't duck my next question.

"Did you mean that? About not letting me down? Or was it just a strategy?"

"What do you think?" he says. Not teasing. Serious. I have to look away.

"You're a good man, Dante," I say quietly, giving the hammock a little push. We rock slowly. Heat shimmers across the pale green lawn that stretches between my house and the Gnome Home. A van pulls into Nonna's driveway, stopping just short of the stacks of boxes Michael and I have dragged from the garage.

"Company," Michael comments.

"It's Diane," I say. I stick one foot out, putting the brakes on the hammock, and somehow detangle myself from the ropes without dumping Michael in the dirt.

"Excuse me? Did I miss something here?" he says, eyes wide. "You are speaking to Diane?" I just give the hammock a playful shove that sets him swinging in answer.

"I'll explain when I get back," I reply, walking toward the house, still holding my glass. "Don't go away."

Little does Michael realize that I couldn't answer his question even if I tried. I'm not sure to what extent I am "speaking" to Diane. She's just come to collect.

It shouldn't have surprised me. Shouldn't have surprised me to see "Diane Pelletier, madeleine pans" written on Nonna's list. But there it was, sure enough. So Mom called Mrs. Pelletier. We scrubbed the pans and wrapped them in tissue paper, like they were gifts. We arranged a time for the Pelletiers to stop by. This afternoon. As I cross the lawn, I see Diane emerge from the van. I take a deep breath.

"Hey," I say as I approach.

"Hey back," she says. "Hot enough for you?"

"Don't kid yourself," I reply. "This is Maine. It'll probably snow next week."

"True," she says. She stands awkwardly alongside the van door. I wonder if we'll keep talking about the weather.

"How's it goin'?" she asks.

"Oh. You know. It's pretty sucky right now," I say.

"Yeah," she sighs. "I'll bet." There is genuine sympathy in her voice. We haven't spoken since Nonna died. Diane and her mom came to the funeral, but it was too crowded for us to say much then. Just a hug, a hurried I'm-so-sorry. Brief and surreal.

"Why don't you come inside?" I say. "We have lemonade."

Diane follows me into the Gnome Home kitchen, which is cluttered with half-full cardboard boxes. Pots and dishes are stacked on the counters.

"Wow," she says. "You guys are already packing up?"

"The owner wants to rent it to someone else." I shrug. I open the fridge, which is empty except for the lemonade. I pour a glass for Diane. "It's good, in a way. Keeps us busy. Especially Mr. Beady." I hand her the glass and take a long, cool sip from mine.

"Brett, I'm so sorry," Diane says, her eyes locked on me.

"Thanks," I reply honestly. "She was the most amazing person I've ever known."

We're quiet for a minute, until I gesture toward the wrapped pans on the counter.

"I'm glad she wanted you to have those," I say. "No one else could do them justice."

"I'll bet you could learn," Diane says. "Are you sure you want me to take them?"

"Absolutely," I say. "Only you have to agree to one thing. The first batch you make? You have to share them with us."

Diane smiles. "Absolutely," she repeats. "We'll have a madeleine party. In honor of Nonna."

"Just one other thing," I add. Mischievously. I can't resist. "Can we *not* invite Jeanne Anne?"

To my surprise, Diane laughs out loud.

"I think that's something you can count on. Especially since we're not speaking."

"Really?" I ask. "Since when?" I try not to look completely shocked.

"Oh . . . it's a long story. I don't know exactly since when. Let's just say you were right about her." Diane picks up the pans from the counter and begins heading toward the kitchen door. My head buzzes with questions, but it's obvious Diane has said all she's going to about Jeanne Anne. I'll have to interrogate Michael later and find out what he knows.

Just before she walks outside, Diane turns, as if she's forgotten something.

"What did Nonna leave you?" she asks.

"Kind of everything . . . except the madeleine pans," I joke. She laughs softly, shaking her head. "But actually . . . since you've asked . . . check this out."

There are three cardboard boxes stacked near the kitchen door. I open the top one and pull out a notebook and a sheet of paper. The notebook is one of the ordinary, college-ruled spiral variety, unremarkable except the cover has scribbled on it: *Journal 1981*. The rest of the boxes are filled with similar books. Diane's eyes widen.

"She left you her diaries?"

"Every one of them. They start when she was ten years old. They're, like, antiques."

"That is *so* cool," Diane says. "Have you read any of them?"

I shake my head. "Not yet," I say, then stop. A lump comes to my throat and I can't say anything else. Diane hesitates, then puts one hand on my shoulder and squeezes.

"I'll see you around, Brett," she says. I nod, staring hard at the floor, as Diane leaves. I return the notebook to its carton and place the sheet of paper on top. Before I close the box, I read the words Nonna scrawled on the paper.

"To Brett, the Family Keeper of Stories."

A new defining characteristic, a surprise, one I have never considered myself. But then, that's how definitions work. They come and go, shift and change, and even when they surprise you, you realize they haven't arrived overnight. They come upon you slowly. Like the tides and the seasons. Like new friends. Like maybe old new friends, reconstituted with laughter and tears, and redefining everything.